Forever Friends

EIGHT ON TEN

Enjoy!

R Jay Berry

Forever Friends

EIGHT ON TEN

R. Jay Berry

Xulon Press

Xulon Press
2301 Lucien Way #415
Maitland, FL 32751
407.339.4217
www.xulonpress.com

Scripture quotations taken from the King James Version (KJV) – *public domain.*

Edited by Xulon Press.

Printed in the United States of America.

ISBN-13: 9781545606643

DEDICATION

This book is dedicated to Mrs. Winona Elizabeth Ragle, the woman who was the mother, the trainer, and most importantly, the friend to all of the women who worked at the Dallas County Sheriff's Department. To many of us, she epitomized who we wanted to be when we really grew up and the women we all became after her teachings, after getting to know her, and getting to love her. Sgt. Ragle, or Miss Ragle, was loved by all and will always be greatly missed by her seven friends from the tenth floor.

PROLOGUE

*D*o you remember what your life was like or what you were doing in the year 1976? Do you remember who the president or the vice president of the United States was in that very year? As you think about your answers to these two questions, did your mind wonder back in time and settle on a time that had an impact on your life? Did you think about all of the people you got to know in 1976 at school, at church, or at work?

If, by chance, your thoughts rested on the people you met at a particular place of employment, did you smile or become so angry you had to take a walk to bury the memories deep in your subconscious again? It may be safe to say that so many people could indeed relate to their very first work experience and the profound effect it had on their lives to this very day. It was not so much that these individuals were now earning their own keep in the world or the fact that they were now on Uncle Sam's tax roll that made them happy to be a part of the work industry. No, it was the fact that they found other individuals to relate to that had similar interests.

That is definitely the case for eight women who in 1976 became not just coworkers but also a close-knit family. It was not the job that sealed their bond but their love for one another.

These eight, came from different backgrounds, ethnicities, parts of the city, and age groups, but these differences did not matter to them. Their closeness was, of course, evident at work, but it brought them closer together after work hours. Nothing was off limits. Birthdays, holidays, concerts, weddings, divorces, child-birth—and yes, even funerals—were events that this group did not take for granted. One could say that these eight women loved each other unconditionally then and now. Our story unfolds at the first meeting for these eight women who would become longtime friends, confidants, and—most importantly—family.

Part 1

WHO WAS WHOM

CHAPTER 1

*I*t was a cool and rainy day in Deerman, Texas, where the lives of eight women were about to change on October 1, 1976. Would these changes be for the better or for the worse? Only time would tell.

It was orientation day for the recently employed members of an elite group of individuals who would risk their safety and sanity each and every day. They had been hired as female officers to work on the tenth floor of the Deerman County Sheriff's Department, specifically with the female inmates. They all knew this was a dangerous assignment, but someone had to do it, so why not them?

Many individuals had come through the doors of this sheriff's department in as many years as the department had been in existence, but they chose not to stay long enough to learn the ins and outs of law enforcement let alone bond with their coworkers. However, this was not the case for eight women who not only learned the true meaning of keeping the peace, so to speak, but also how you come to depend on the people you are forced to work with.

"I need the following six individuals to meet Sgt. Ragland at the elevator to begin your county orientation: Astor, Goodman, Edwards, Ogilvie, Simmons, and Woodson. Blank and bewildered looks all registered on the faces of these women when they heard their names called. They all looked in the same direction at the same moment as the sergeant rose from her chair positioned behind the county spokesperson and walked toward the elevator. Her straight back posture and steady long strides showed that the sergeant was a confident woman.

She did not look at any of the women, but it seemed they all sensed she was a no-nonsense person who would not tolerate shirking job responsibility by the quick manner in which they arose from their respective chairs to meet her at the elevator. None of the women recognized each other, but they slowly gathered toward the elevator in anticipation. The women ranged in ages from twenty-two to thirty-five and just as their ages were varied, their heights were just as varied from five foot three inches to five foot eight inches with their weights in proportion to their heights. Standing in silence, the women looked off into space, each trying not to look at each other. Unbeknownst to any of them, their lives had already started to change.

No words were spoken as they all waited for the elevator door to open. All of the women took quick glances at this woman they had not formally been introduced to yet, and her blank expression gave them no clue as to how she would interact with them.

The door opened slowly, and all of the women entered the small room before the door had completely opened. Not a word was spoken as the sergeant pushed button number five. It took what seemed to be an eternity for the door to reclose and just as long for the elevator movement to begin. When they finally reached their destination, the women waited for their appointed leader to take the first step onto this floor.

"Follow me ladies," were the sergeant's first words to the group, and follow her is what they did.

Sgt. Ragland was an Anglo woman approximately five foot six inches tall and weighed about one hundred and sixty pounds. She was one of the first three women to not only be hired to work as matrons at the county, but most importantly, she was the first woman to be promoted to the sergeant rank. She was put in charge of working on the tenth floor where the female prisoners were housed. Sgt. Ragland excelled at her job as well as being an excellent training officer. What the ladies would soon find out was that all of the officers at the sheriff's department, but especially the female officers, looked up to the sergeant because of her dedication to her job, her title, and the training she provided for her female trainees. This was day one of many days together for these unsuspecting fledglings that would one day fly on their own at the Deerman County Sheriff's Department.

CHAPTER 2

*A*ll of the ladies took a seat without being asked but not on row one but all on row two. Not knowing what to expect, they had all thought to themselves better to be further away and out of the line of fire. Figuring out their fear, the sergeant took a few steps and stood in front of the ladies on the second row which made her closer to them than if they had selected seats on the first row.

"Ladies, my name is Sgt. Winifred Ragland and I will be your training officer. As I call your name please reseat yourselves in alpha order on the first row. Astor, Edwards, Goodman, Ogilvie, Simmons, and Woodson."

The ladies quickly stood and as they were about to be reseated after name call, the sergeant said, "Officer Laura Hill will be joining us later this morning, so for paperwork's sake she will be between officers Goodman and Ogilvie."

These two officers looked at each other, and by the bewildered looks on their faces, they both wondered why this officer Hill was not here with them now.

4

"I need to complete some paperwork and submit it to the lieutenant, so while I am gone, get to know your fellow officers. These individuals will not just be your coworkers; they will become the people that you will learn to trust the most. You will have each other's backs at all times. Officers, the operative word here is *will*. I am sure I do not have to repeat this lesson."

The ladies looked at each other, and it was evident that they had not formed an opinion about their training officer yet, but they were sure she was a no-nonsense leader.

With those statements, the sergeant turned her back and left the ladies to fend for themselves. What they did not know was this was their first assignment and test given by their training officer. Leaving on the pretense of seeing the lieutenant, the sergeant was actually watching the ladies through a two-way mirror from the next room. She wanted to see how they followed directives, how they interacted with each other, but mostly, what approach she needed to take with these strangers if there was not an instant gelling.

As the door closed behind the sergeant, the room was silent for about two minutes. Then, Officer Simmons was the first to rise from her seat and formally introduce herself to her fellow officers. "Hello everyone. My name is Rita Simmons, and I just graduated a few months ago with a degree in psychology. This is the perfect job for me because it will allow me to rehabilitate the prisoners."

Her fellow officers looked at her with strange expressions and slight smiles on their faces. They all saw a young, thin, and attractive impressionable-looking black woman who did not look like she could hurt a fly. She was about five feet seven and a half inches tall and weighed about one hundred and five pounds. Needless to say, Officer Simmons would not intimidate anyone with her small stature, but maybe her mind would put prisoners on the straight and narrow path.

Rita began her introduction: "I am from a middle class family and I am the oldest of four children. My parents sacrificed a lot to give us the best education possible. I graduated from an all-girls high school and then decided to go to an all-girls university. When I finally decided on my college major of psychology, I had every intention of using this knowledge to help the world. So when I got the job at the sheriff's department, I knew this was my opportunity and calling."

Rita was a trusting soul who saw the good in everyone. Some would say she was naïve because she felt this way, but that is also why everyone liked her: her innocence.

"This is my first real job and I am so excited to be here. I can't wait to get started," she stated with a big smile.

Officer Edwards was the first to reply to Rita's job-related revelation.

"In all of my years of police work, I don't think prisoners can be rehabilitated, Rita, but maybe you will have better luck than anyone I know."

All of the ladies chuckled softly, including Rita, and she was feeling more at ease. It was evident that Rita Simmons was in for a life lesson that would help her literally grow up well beyond her twenty-two years. Officer Edwards smiled at Rita, offered her hand to her with a big smile on her face, and just like that, the first two friends had emerged.

CHAPTER 3

The second introduction began with Gigi. "Hello everyone, my name is Gigi Edwards. I know what that name sounds like, but my mother saw a movie with Maurice Chevalier and his wife's name in the movie was Gigi, and it stuck. My mother told me when she heard it she knew that had to be my name. I guess it's not so bad, but I got a lot of ribbing in school, especially from the girls. They always told me no white mother in her right mind would name their daughter Gigi as her real name." Gigi laughed as did the other officers as she continued talking. Unlike Rita, Gigi looked confident and sure of herself.

"I have been working in various locations in the jail but never in detentions. My husband Evan and daughter Monica and I just moved here from Camden, Texas. Evan got transferred down here to work in the crime lab in Deerman. I started not to come with him since I do not see myself married to the man much longer, but Monica wanted to be near her grandmother Lois, my mother, who lives about an hour away from us in Fairfield."

Gigi told the group how she had married Evan right out of high school and soon after had their daughter Monica. Apparently, Evan had changed over the years, and even though he was in law enforcement, had committed some crimes of his own that made Gigi not trust him anymore.

Gigi could be described as an attractive shapely woman with a walk that most men loved and drooled over. Her walk was one of those walks that you saw models learn how to do when they walked the runway in fashion shows. The only difference was that they had to be taught how to walk that way, and Gigi already knew the model walk.

Her five-foot, four-inch frame was well proportioned, and she was very knowledgeable about life surrounding the inner workings of law enforcement. During her brief description about her life and law enforcement experience from her jobs and her husband, Gigi explained she had seen many crimes being committed and crimes being solved.

"My husband thinks this transfer to Deerman is going to make things better with our marriage, but I am not hopeful, but he doesn't know that yet." Rita thought, *That's a lot of information. My life must seem boring compared to Gigi's life. I don't have anything like that to share with the group.* The other ladies smiled, and you could sense the ice beginning to break as they took their turns and offered information about their respective lives.

"Okay, now everyone knows about my torrid life, who's next?" asked Gigi.

CHAPTER 4

"*D*oes anybody know where I can get a diet Dr. Pepper?" was the next comment made. Everyone looked at this officer and replied no, so she continued with her introduction.

"Hi y'all, I'm Poppi Astor, and the first thing you need to know about me is I love diet Dr. Pepper. Second, if you're wondering about my name, my mother likes flowers, especially poppies." All of the ladies laughed at Poppi's comments.

"Most people call me Pop for short but that could also be because I love me some diet Dr. Pepper. If you ever want to get on my good side just bring me a diet Dr. Pepper.

Everyone had now turned their attention to Poppi and her self-description.

"I know I need to lose about five pounds and then I can at least wear my tight jeans when I go to the rodeo."

Poppi was about five feet five inches tall and looked to weigh about one hundred fifteen pounds. All of her fellow officers commented on how wonderful they thought she looked and saw no reason why she should be trying to lose any weight.

"Well, all I can say is that you do not need to lose any weight, but I need to shed about five to ten pounds," replied Gigi.

Gigi and Poppi were about the same height, but Poppi wore glasses and had a continuous smile on her face.

"I am from a small town near Corsicana, Texas and I just completed two years of college. I knew that was enough schooling for me so I decided to join the Deerman sheriff's department. I don't know about rehabilitating prisoners; I just know I needed a job."

Everyone laughed at her comment. During Poppi's brief introduction, she walked to the front of the room and everyone noticed her brisk walk that made you believe she was a fast learner or maybe she just needed her diet Dr. Pepper. She and Gigi seemed to hit it off since it seemed that Corsicana was not that far from Fairfield, and they had discovered in this brief communication that they knew some of the same people.

"Okay, I am not married, nor do I have a boyfriend. So if any of you know of a nice young man, I am available. By the way, I do not go out with married men who say they are single." All smiled at Poppi's frankness.

"If they ask what type of person I am, just tell them I like rodeos and country-western dancing, but I love going to clubs and dinner. Okay, who's next on the get to know our fellow officers list?" asked Poppi.

CHAPTER 5

"*I* guess I am," said Joy Ogilvie. Joy was the only officer who did not see the humor in the conversation that had been taking place thus far. She appeared to be a serious-minded woman. Rita offered her hand to Joy and with a smile asked the question, "What do you like to do for fun, Joy?"

"Not much. I like to read and sleep when and where I can. I am from Hershey, Pennsylvania and no, I do not have any connections with the Hershey chocolate factory to get anyone free chocolate. Now with that out of the way, as you can see, I am taller than Gigi and Poppi but not as tall as Rita and I probably weigh more than Gigi but for sure more than Poppi, and I want to look more like Rita, but I really do not care at this point in my life."

All of the other ladies took a deep breath for Joy as she continued with her life's tale.

"I am not married and do not foresee that happening in my future anytime soon. By the way, as you can tell, I like to get right to the point. I have a brother and three sisters, and we still talk to each other occasionally. My mother named me Joy because I am

12

always the life of the party I guess, even before I was born. I am not over friendly to people I do not know, and I take my time getting to know everyone. Oh, by the way, another small tidbit about myself. My family calls me Anne because they think I act like Princess Anne. I have never found any humor in this but whatever. This is me—Joy or Anne—take it or leave it.

"On another note, I used to work for Budweiser delivering beer to restaurants. I do not have any contacts for free beer either, so don't even think about asking for that." With that, Joy took her seat next to Rita, who smiled at her. Joy gave her a smallish smile in return. *I really like her, thought Rita.* As Gigi appeared to be the spokesperson of the group, she was the first to speak.

"Well, we all know who our pit bull will be if we need one." All of the officers including Joy chuckled at that statement. No more icebergs were in this room.

CHAPTER 6

"*M*oving along, next, whose next? asked Gigi." When not one of the remaining ladies responded, Gigi looked at the next candidate on the list, officer Woodson. "Okay officer you're up. Tell us about your darkest secrets. We need some dirt right about now," smiled Gigi.

"Oh Lord," replied officer Woodson. "Well, my name is Rose Woodson, and my husband Brian and I have four children—two girls and two boys. I stay busy with the kids, but I needed this job to help ends meet. Looking at all of you, I think it's safe to say I am the oldest in the bunch." She smiled at her fellow officers who were all standing with smiles on their faces as well. You could tell they were all waiting to hear how old she was.

"Okay, I am thirty five, so there. I was a late bloomer. I had all of these kids, and they started eating more and needing more things, so Brian and I decided it was time for me to go back to work. By the way, I know I need to lose some weight but I do not have time. It's all of these kids. I used to look like Rita, but that was before I had child number one. But one thing I can do is cook. My specialty is chicken and dumplings. The kids and Brian love it. Brian works at an automotive shop selling parts to dealerships, so we get a lot of our car parts for free. My kids are fifteen, thirteen, eleven, and eight. Now that they are old enough to stay alone in the evenings until Brian gets home, I can work this job. Now that's out of the way." It appeared that was a load off her shoulder's because she immediately began fanning.

"Boy it's hot in here," Rose commented as she took her seat.

"I would love to taste some of your chicken and dumplings," replied Rita. Rose felt more comfortable about maybe becoming the sage officer in the group regarding family and cooking. It was evident, Rose had information they could all use and learn from.

"Okay Miss Rose," Gigi said. "So when we have our first get-together, you will be expected to bring some home cooking. We can decide on the menu later," she responded, smiling. All Rose could say with a smile was, "Oh, Lord."

CHAPTER 7

The last of the introductions was reluctantly started by the last of the new recruits, Madyson Goodman. Officer Goodman was a small-framed twenty-four-year-old woman who was also married and the mother of two small children. Her brunette hair did not have a strand out of place, and her makeup was carefully done. Her two-toned eye shadow colors looked good on the outside, but there was a sadness behind the color.

With cigarette in hand, she began her short introduction after taking a long puff as if to give herself courage to begin her conversation. "My name is Madyson, but my friends call me Maddy, but my husband shortened it to Mad. I think my husband sometimes thinks I am insane, and I guess I have to agree with him.

I got this job because my husband drives me nuts, so I am mad, in a sense. My husband is a fireman and gone most of the time, so I have to take care of most things in the house as well as the kids, so I needed a break. Don't get me wrong, I love my kids dearly, and they are my refuge. A little confused, Rose had to ask, "So who is taking care of your kids now?"

"I put them in a daycare so I need this job to pay for the day-care. If I could bring them with me I would." No one replied at this moment but Rita thought, *Madyson seems a little sad and it appears she is looking for something more in her life.* The first psychological observation by the resident psychologist had been made, and it was not even of an inmate. Go figure. There were no smiles when Madyson spoke of her husband, so maybe this new group of women had something for her ails. With that, Madyson returned to her puffing without another word about her life. Not sure how to proceed after this latest revelation by Madyson, the room was quiet.

"Ladies, I think we need to schedule our first outing," Gigi recommended.

"I also think Madyson should be our official group entertainment representative."

"I agree with that," said Rose. "She and I can get together on the food and what I need to cook."

"I think I can manage that," Madyson replied after she took another puff from her cigarette. "The first one can be at my house. I can get my next-door neighbor to babysit, and my husband will be working nights for the next month."

All of the officers seemed to agree with Gigi's assessment of the situation and her resolution to continued comradery outside of the workplace. However, before they could discuss first time place and time particulars, the elevator door opened and Sgt. Ragland briskly stepped out.

The officers returned to their assigned seats and looked and listened attentively to their new leader.

CHAPTER 8

"*L*adies, I will now pass out information about your uniforms and where you can order them as well as your working schedule for the next six weeks. Please complete any necessary information in your packets and be ready to turn this in when you return from lunch. We will now break for lunch, but please return back to this room in one hour from now. At that point, I will answer any questions you may have and then we will go to the tenth floor for the rest of our orientation.

As Sgt. Ragland left the room again, the officers gathered their belongings and decided where they would go for lunch. "Wonder where Officer Hill is?" asked Gigi. Maybe she decided not to join us after all," Madyson surmised.

As the new female officers of the Deerman County Sheriff's Department returned promptly in one hour from their first of many lunches, they all met back in the same room where they first initially met each other. Sgt. Ragland was not in the room when they arrived, but little did they know that this was their second test. So far, the ladies had passed their two tests with flying colors. They knew each other, and they were punctual.

In about ten minutes, the door opened and the ladies went to their respective temporary seats and waited for further instructions from Sgt. Ragland.

"Officers do any of you have any questions for me before we go to the Commerce Building?"

All of the officers looked at each other, but no one had any questions.

"If there are no questions, we will now continue our meeting on the tenth floor of the Commerce Building. If you have had an opportunity to review your work schedule, you will notice that you have all been assigned to work on the tenth floor where the female inmates are housed. During your probationary period of six months, you will be trained on what it means to be a female detention officer, which means the dos and don'ts of law enforcement. Again, I ask if any of you have any questions. If not now, you may have some questions after we get to the tenth floor and you see where you will be working regarding the ins and outs of the jail. With that, please follow me to the tenth floor."

All of the ladies were anxious to see their new job location. Not knowing what to expect, the ladies followed the sergeant in complete silence, making sure not to miss any vital sights on the way. Sgt. Ragland walked the ladies through many different departments on their journey and the officers saw firsthand what a large operation this law enforcement gig truly was. All seemed amazed except Gigi, who already knew a lot about the workings of the departments within a jail.

"Hello Sgt. Ragland," was spoken by all of those that they came in contact with the sergeant, which made the ladies see just how respected their new sergeant was. It appeared that she was liked by all. There was even a brief hello by Sheriff Karlton Thompson, who had stepped out of his office to speak to his secretary during this time.

"Hello, sergeant. Our new officer recruits, I see, sergeant," remarked Sheriff Thompson.

"Yes, sir. First day on the job," was the response from the sergeant.

After this short exchange of words, it was evident that some of the officers had perplexed looks on their faces because they saw the sheriff up close and personal their very first day, but they did not say a word at this time.

This experience was so new for all of the officers because it was evident there was much to learn. But as they would soon find out, they had an excellent teacher and mentor. As they left the busy bond desk area, they were led to what was called number one turnkey. This is where our ladies get their first glimpse of the inner workings of the jail.

"Hello Officer Hamilton. You doing alright today?"

"Yes, Sgt. Ragland. All is good."

"Hamilton these are our new detention officers for the tenth floor. I am taking them up there now so they can get to know the jail a little bit. Ladies, sign in here so we can proceed."

"Sergeant, we are so glad they are finally here. We need the help," was Hamilton's response.

"There is an Officer Hill already here and is waiting for you on the prisoners' bench by turnkey number three."

"Yes, I know, thank you Hamilton." The officers looked at each other because they were all wondering what had happened to Officer Hill. Officer Hamilton welcomed the new officers, and they all responded with a resounding thank you. After they signed in, they continued on their new journey.

CHAPTER 9

The inner workings of the jail were now unfolding for our six officers. There were actual prisoners in plain view now. Some were shining shoes, others were mopping the floor, and still others were being booked into jail. However, while there were a large number of prisoners visible, there were even more officers in sight to watch all of the prisoners. So much was going on. The ladies would soon find out these prisoners were called trustees because for whatever the reason, they were trusted outside of their cells to perform certain jobs in the jail.

Gigi was a very outgoing and bubbly person and was the only one who was speaking to the other officers when she passed them as though she already knew them. "Ya'll, we're gonna like working here," she whispered to her new friends.

As the sergeant led the ladies closer to the elevator to get to the tenth floor, they saw a woman sitting on the concrete bench at the end of the hallway. The woman was sitting there with her legs crossed, cigarette in hand, and a stoic look on her face. When the sergeant reached the bench destination, the woman slowly rose and introduced herself as Laura Hill. All of her fellow officers looked at her, but no one spoke.

"This is Officer Hill ladies," was the introduction from the sergeant.

"You all can introduce yourselves after we get upstairs."

Low murmurs of hellos were exchanged by all, and they all proceeded to get on the elevator.

As the elevator door was closing, a woman's voice was heard saying, "Hold the elevator please." The sergeant hit the open door button, and there appeared a woman dressed all in white with a big smile on her face.

"Thank you, Sgt. Ragland," she spoke. "Hello Miss Nurse—I mean Miss Traci. Ladies this is Traci Hodges, one of the nurses who works here in the jail. We call Traci Miss Nurse because the prisoners like her so much. They love to see Miss Nurse coming to see them every day."

"Hello ladies. Is this your first day?"

"Yes," was the response given by all.

"Great. So glad you are here."

The elevator door finally closed, and the tenth floor experience was finally underway. Our young psychology graduate was so overwhelmed that she was overheard saying a few words of thanks to the Lord. No one acknowledged her comments or made her feel uncomfortable, but at this moment, they had learned something new about Officer Rita Simmons.

CHAPTER 10

*A*s the ladies reached the tenth floor and stepped from the elevator, all was quiet on the floor with the female inmates as well as the officers.

"Good luck today ladies," said Miss Nurse and she proceeded to go to the tenth floor control center, as it was called by the officers, so she could be escorted to the hospital to check on these inmates first.

Sgt. Ragland escorted the officers to the control center and introduced them to Officers Turnby and Rhinna who were currently working on the floor. The third officer working this shift was Flawsen but she was not readily available during these initial introductions, but they would all meet her soon. Officer Turnby escorted Miss Nurse to the hospital to begin her medication distribution for all of the female inmates.

At this point, Officer Flawsen appeared in the control center carrying a brief case that she soon put away. She seemed nice enough, but there was something about Flawsen that was evident to the ladies. They would soon find out that their new fellow officer by a mere three months was different.

"Ladies, we will meet in the shakedown room for a brief moment before we begin our tour of the floor. Follow me," Sgt. Ragland commented.

All of the ladies did just that and followed their sergeant into the room where new prisoners to the floor were taken to be searched and given their new jail attire before going to their cell.

As they made their way into the shakedown room, they all witnessed the room that would become very familiar to all of them. The sergeant asked them to all sit down and wait for her as she relieved the three officers as their shift ended and greeted the next shift of officers as their shift began. While this was not another test per se, this was the opportunity for them to formally meet Officer Hill.

"Okay ya'll let's meet our last comrade while the Sarg is out of the room. Let me see if I remember everyone's information. First, I am Gigi Edwards and I worked at the Camden Police department. Next, this is our resident psychologist Rita Simmons. She is our recent college graduate so be careful; she will analyze you." There was laughter by all.

"Next we have Poppi Astor who was named after a flower and has a passion for diet Dr. Pepper."

"That is the most important fact you will hear today," Poppi said.

"Okay let's see. Oh yes, we have our own built in pit bull Joy Ogilvie. Joy is a no nonsense person, but while I personally think that is an act, we will see. Rose Woodson is the cook in the bunch with four kids. She will probably try to mother all of us, but as long as she can cook, we will accept her mothering."

"Oh Lord," commented Rose over the laughter of everyone else.

"Last but not least we have Madyson Goodman who took this job because her husband was driving her nuts. She has already agreed to be our entertainment representative, and our first gathering will be at her house. No one corrected Gigi's short introductions of her fellow five officers so now they all looked at Officer Hill, who was taking all of this in sitting on the bench with her legs crossed. "Okay, Hill, your turn," Gigi commented.

Officer Hill was approximately five feet ten inches tall and weighed about one hundred fifty pounds. She seemed very confident and like a take-charge person. Still with her legs crossed and smoking her cigarette she started her formal introduction speaking in a low monotone voice.

"I worked for the Dartmouth Police Department for four years as a patrol officer. I am getting married to my fiancé Donald soon at the Horticultural Center in the Fair Park. My older sister Barbara and my mother Doris are my family, and we are very close."

There were no smiles during this short excerpt from Laura Hill, but it was evident there was also a certain kind of respect from the other officers as they listened to the way she spoke.

There was a silence at this moment because no one knew how to proceed. As everyone was searching for the words to say, Sgt. Ragland came back into the shakedown room.

"Okay ladies, I assume you all have met Officer Hill, so now I can complete my initial speech to you now that you are all here. First of all, you are from this moment forward officers who work at the Deerman County Sheriff's Department. You, as well as every officer in the sheriff's department, represent the sheriff, whether you are in your uniform or not and wherever you go.

The reason I wanted to make sure you knew a little something about each other is because you seven ladies are now more than officers. You are now sisters in every sense of the word. You have each other's back in all situations, and if one needs help, you all go to the rescue without question. This directive is non negotiable. When you work this tenth floor, these prisoners will do whatever it takes to escape or cause you to make mistakes to get them released. You have to always communicate with each other, and there is no such thing as you not getting along with each other. This is a dangerous job. You will be babysitting criminals of all sorts. They will smile in your face each day to gain your confidence and make you think they are your friends all the while trying to escape or harm you. Remember, they are criminals, not your friends. Your only friends on this floor will be each of you. Now, let's begin our tour of the floor. Take mental notes because this is intensive on-the-job training. Now, follow me closely and listen up."

The officers looked at each other but no words were spoken but they immediately followed their sergeant.

"Wonder what the sergeant's story is," Gigi whispered to Poppi, but everyone heard her question.

By looking at the sergeant, you could tell by her light hair color she had probably been a true blond in her younger days, but the few strands of gray had changed her hair color to a darker color of blond. The new trainees would soon find out that she was a single mother of two and the sole provider for her children since her beloved husband's death, and she never missed a day of work. Tough but fair was how her officers would come to characterize her.

As the new officers gave their new sergeant the once-over, several things were noticed by all of them but verbalized by Gigi.

"Do you notice her pink manicured nails?" Gigi whispered to Poppi.

"I see them, replied Poppi. Do you see how nice her hair is styled? Not a hair out of place. I bet it's always like that."

Part 2

ON-THE-JOB TRAINING

Chapter 11

"*I* have asked the officers from the evening shift to stay in the office while I show each of you where the cells are located, how to use the keys, and how to go with the nurse to dispense medication. Ladies, this is Officer Flawsen. She, like you, is still on probation and has been here almost four months. Please hand me the hospital keys, Flawsen," Sgt. Ragland requested.

Everyone said their hellos to the not-so-new trainee who looked as if she wanted to be anywhere but where she was. As soon as the sergeant and her trainees left the control center, Poppi noticed Flawsen taking a briefcase back into the bathroom.

"Did you see Flawsen with that briefcase? Somethings strange about her, said Poppi. "Why do you carry a briefcase with you to work in the jail and then in the restroom?"

No one else made a statement, but they all noticed the shiny bright black patent leather briefcase.

"First, we will go to the hospital so you can see the prisoners there. Make no mistake, they are in the hospital because they have an ailment that requires constant attention, but they are first and foremost prisoners.

Did you all hear about the lady who supposedly murdered her husband and daughter because they made her wait to eat dinner? Well, Margo Meadowstone is her name, and that is her speaking to Miss Nurse. Margo is sentenced to go on trial in a few months. She appears like anyone's grandmother who bakes cookies all day, but she is a cold-blooded murderer. Always be on alert when you are around her. Any questions so far?"

No one had any questions, but looks of disbelief, fear, and amazement appeared on their faces at different times. They were all listening attentively and taking in all of this pertinent information, and Sgt. Ragland was not holding back any details. She was speaking from her knowledge and experience and had no notes or reminders. All of the officers were trying to remember her words, and while they asked no questions, there were definite deer-in-the-headlights looks.

One of the officers in the control center came to tell Sgt. Ragland that Rosa Lynn was at it again and asking to see her. She immediately stopped her conversation with her trainees and headed down the hallway. The trainees followed her, anxious to see who this person was that their sergeant would literally stop her conversation mid-sentence to head in the opposite direction.

"Rosa Lynn, what is going on?" Sgt. Ragland asked her.

"Sgt. Ragland, I didn't get my letta' mailed today. Those other officers took my letta' and burned it. I saw them burn my letta' to my sons. My boys is waiting on that letta'."

"Rosa Lynn, why is your mattress wet? What did you do?"

"Miss Sergeant, I didn't do nothing. Those other lady officers threw water on my mattress so I couldn't write another letta'. They wet up my mattress so I couldn't sleep. Can you get my letta' back? My sons, they worried 'bout me."

"Rosa Lynn, what is that smell? Have you been saving some fluids again?"

The officers all looked at each other with the same questions written on their faces.

"What does that mean?" asked Rita?

"I am sure Sgt. Ragland is asking her about fluids that should be flushed down the toilet," replied Gigi.

Rita looked as though she had seen a ghost in the jail.

"Miss Sergeant, those other officers wet my mattress with water from the mop bucket. They is trying to stop me from writin' my lettas'."

Sgt. Ragland looked perturbed at Rosa Lynn, quickly left the cell, and walked back to the control center. The officers could tell by her tone that the sergeant was not happy, but she never raised her voice to Rosa Lynn or any of the other officers in the control center. The ladies all noticed that their leader was most assuredly upset, but her tone levels never increased above her normal talking voice.

R. Jay Berry

They would soon come to realize that Sgt. Ragland was tough, and that toughness was greatly appreciated. Her expectations were that all of her officers would report to work in a timely manner every day, perform their job while at work, and treat all of the prisoners as just that, prisoners. All of these messages were quickly learned by the officers because they were reinforced every day.

Chapter 12

"Ladies, let us get back to the hospital, Sgt. Ragland commented remarked.

"We will discuss Rosa Lynn later today. There are special things you all need to know about her before you can begin work."

With that, all of the officers followed their fearless leader back to the hospital in total silence.

"As I was saying, always be on alert when going into the hospital. These inmates are all in the hospital for a reason, but first and foremost, illness or no illness, if they thought they could escape or take your keys or even hurt you, they would. Never, and I repeat never, let your guard down around any prisoner, especially those in the hospital. The closer they get to their trial dates or being sent to prison, the more they will act out or try to get on your good side. One day I came to the hospital with Miss Nurse to dispense medication and when we arrived at the door we noticed that Margo was lying on the floor motionless."

All of the trainees were hypnotized by Sgt. Ragland's words. It was as though they were in a haunted house, fearful to go upstairs because of what they might find or see.

"As we opened the hospital door, Margo still lay motionless on the floor. All of the other inmates were gathered around her as though they were in shock at her condition as well. I told Miss Nurse to stand behind me and let me take control of the situation. Glad to comply, Miss Nurse never moved from the doorway. Before I entered the hospital area, I told the other inmates to get back to their beds immediately. I noticed that none of them tried to offer an explanation to me of what had happened, so I knew this was probably a ploy by Margo—and really all of the inmates—to make us think she had collapsed and needed immediate medical attention.

"If I had not been on my toes, I would have rushed in alone unprepared and would have been overtaken by all of these inmates. I looked all around the hospital to see if I noticed anything that was out of place. Then I saw where Margo had torn apart a box of Kotex next to her bed to get the cotton inside. I immediately looked at Margo and saw how swollen her face looked, and at this point, I turned around and walked back to Miss Nurse and instructed her to go and get the emergency paddles and call Lieutenant Knobles and ask him to bring some male officers from the twelfth floor to help transport her body in the event she died and needed to be moved to another floor before being sent to the morgue. I then made sure I locked the door behind her and made sure all of the inmates heard me say that it looked as though Margo had what looked like a heart attack."

All of the officers were speechless. They couldn't wait to hear how this tale ended.

"At this moment, Margo's eyes began to flutter and she started to move her body. I did not unlock the hospital door or seem excited to see that Margo who was still lying on the floor and was now appearing lucid and beginning to move on her own. I saw her spit something from her mouth and saw it was the cotton.

"At this moment, the elevator door opened and Lieutenant Knobles walked from the elevator with five male officers from the twelfth floor all prepared to do whatever needed to be done. The lieutenant knew that this was not the correct protocol established to handle inmates who are legitimately sick or need immediate attention, but ladies, my point in telling you this story was to make sure you all always remember how important it is to be alert when around all of these inmates, even the trustees. They are criminals first and foremost. I spoke to the lieutenant for a few minutes, and he understood the situation, so he and the other officers left the floor.

"Nothing was said to Margo about this stunt, but she went for one month without making her supervised weekly phone call and no commissary. Commissary is where the inmates can purchase items like cigarettes and other toiletries from Rob the commissary man once a week. The inmates always look forward to him coming."

CHAPTER 13

*A*ll of the officers listened attentively and seemed amazed at this story. Sgt. Ragland finished showing her new officers the lay of the jail workings, always with profound messages for them to remember.

It was time for the next shift to begin, and promptly at 2:30 the elevator door opened, and three new officers emerged to work the evening shift. All of the introductions were completed with these officers and like clockwork the morning shift officers were passing on vital information about their shift as well as the keys to all of the cells.

After briefing the evening shift officers, Rhinna and Turnby were preparing to leave when the sergeant asked where Officer Flawsen was. At this moment, Flawsen came from the restroom, again carrying that same briefcase, and it was evident she had on a new shade of lipstick and different color eye shadow.

"Flawsen I need to speak to you in the shakedown room immediately," were the words Sgt. Ragland spoke at this moment.

Not seeming too excited at this request, Flawsen took her time and followed the sergeant as she had requested. While the sergeant was gone the new officers introduced themselves to officers Hamilton, Valens, and Proctor, who would be working the evening shift, and they were all singing Sgt. Ragland's praises. But they all concurred and spoke the same words: "As long as you do your job, the sergeant is a wonderful supervisor," Turnby noted. "She never raises her voice, but make no mistake, you will know when she is upset. Everyone loves Sgt. Ragland."

At this moment, the door to the shakedown room opened, and while last going in, Flawsen was the first to come out and not in a good mood. She did not say a word to anyone and walked straight to the elevator, pushed the button, and when the door opened, she got in and did not wait on the rest of her fellow officers.

"You see what I mean," one of the officers whispered.

The morning shift officers said their good byes and again told the new officers how glad they were to meet them and left the floor. For the rest of the day, Sgt. Ragland took the new trainees to each floor to meet the other officers, who were mostly male, and the supervisors on each floor.

This was indeed a long day for the new officers on ten.

"Ladies, there is much to learn, and it will take a while to learn the ins and outs of all of the floors and what needs to be done on each shift. You will all begin working your normal shifts beginning with the midnight shift tomorrow night. You will be on each shift for six weeks and you will change to days, then evenings, and then back to midnights. You will be responsible for getting your uniforms ordered, but in the meantime, until they come in, you can wear comfortable dark pants, black shoes, and plain shirts with no writing or symbols on them. It takes about four weeks to get your uniforms, and in your packets, the location of where you go to order them is enclosed.

"I expect you all to be here tomorrow night before your shift starts for a briefing with all of the officers before each shift to get your assignments for that shift. These briefings take place in the shakedown room on the second floor behind the lieutenant's office before each shift. I will show each of you where this room is located when we go down. So if your shift begins at 10:30 P.M., you need to arrive no later than 10:00 P.M. For now, all of you will be assigned to the tenth floor, but on occasion you will have other assignments in the turnkeys and other floors."

The ladies all looked at each other not sure what these assignments entailed. No one asked a question, but there were definite puzzled looks on their faces.

"Ladies it will take you all a while to get to know the workings of the jail even if you have some experience already. My expectations are that you will learn it all together and help each other and always come to me if you have questions about anything. Now, no one expects you to learn all of this overnight, but you will be expected to go that extra mile to prove that you deserve to be here.

I am sure you all know you are all on six months' probation. What that means is you need to follow the jail rules and my rules all of the time. Any questions?"

None of the ladies responded with a question so the sergeant rode the elevator with them back to the second floor and, as promised, showed them the shakedown room.

"It smells in here," whispered Simmons.

All of the ladies agreed with her by way of a nod, but they could tell the sergeant was used to this smell. As there were no questions, they received their packets with all of the vital information they needed, which included their respective days off.

"Ladies, read this information carefully and for those of you who will be working tomorrow night, I will see you then. Looks like that will be Edwards, Ogilvie, Simmons, and Woodson. See you all tomorrow night.

With that, the ladies were dismissed and all met in the cafeteria for a brief meeting of their own. This would be the first of many meetings for these ladies.

CHAPTER 14

O
n October 1, 1976, between 9:30 and 10:00 P.M. the next night, officers Edwards, Ogilvie, Simmons, and Woodson arrived for their first day and night of many at the Deerman County Sheriff's Department. Officer Simmons was the first to arrive for her first full-time job since graduating with her psychology degree. She felt so lost and alone even with this degree. *How could she possibly help anyone if she was too afraid to speak what she thought?*

As she walked back to the area where Sgt. Ragland showed them the day before, no one said a word to her, maybe because they did not know she was an officer since she did not have her uniform yet. But she knew she had that officer air about her. As she got closer to her designated area, she saw Lt. Williams, who seemed to recognize her.

"Hello Officer Simmons, he commented.

"Hello sir, was all that she could mouth.

She walked into the shakedown room, and no one was there yet, so she decided to sit on the hard concrete bench outside of the Lieutenant's office. She later found out that this was also where the prisoners sat before they went up to the floors. Simmons heard a familiar voice that took her attention from the hardness of this bench. She saw Edwards walking towards her and speaking to everyone along the way. Clerks, officers, and prisoners were all greeted the same. Simmons noticed she had a confident walk and demeanor that she envied.

"Hi doctor, is how Edwards greeted Simmons.

"Hi Gigi. Do you know any of those people you were speaking to?"

"No, never met any of them." *I need to be more outgoing like Gigi, she thought.* As it got to the actual work time, more officers were appearing. Rita was taking all of this movement in, and at this very moment she saw an officer that made her heart start to beat faster. She began to perspire and her hands became clammy.

Not sure what was going on, she spotted one male officer dressed in his khaki uniform in a sea of khaki attired male officers reporting to work that caught more than her attention. She was mesmerized by this male officer. At the very moment they made eye contact, she was sure she heard a bell. Rita thought she was hearing things because it was evident no one else heard this bell.

There he stood, this brown colored not-so-tall man with a perfect shaped afro. He was beyond cute. *He is downright handsome, she thought.* They looked at each other for what seemed like an eternity but was only a few minutes when she noticed him shaking his head and then looking away. At this very moment, Rita made

46

up her mind he was the one, the one she was going to marry. Did this officer in training need more schooling beyond the jail?

"Gigi do you see that cute officer standing there in front of the door at the control center? That one with the cute afro?"

"Which one? Gigi replied.

"The cute one in front with the semi-dimpled smile," was all Rita could say. "The one who is talking to the trustee."

"Yes, I see him. He is cute, responded Gigi. "Only on the job one day, and you already see someone you like."

Gigi chuckled at this revelation so Rita decided to keep the fact to herself that this was her soulmate and her future husband. Maybe this secret could be kept until after she at least knew his first name.

About this time all of her other female comrades and the remaining officers reporting for work had arrived, including Sgt. Ragland. The ladies all huddled together seeing as they didn't know anyone else, although that didn't stop Gigi from meeting whoever she could and making more friends.

About this time, Lt. Williams came out of his office and headed to the shakedown room, and all of the officers followed him in there, including Sgt. Ragland, so it was safe to say this is where the ladies headed as well.

"Today we have several new officers joining the jail ranks today. Sgt. Ragland, would you do the honors, please?"

"Yes, sir," she responded. "Ladies, as I call your name please stand so everyone can put a face with your names. We have officers

Edwards, Ogilvie, Simmons, and Woodson." All of the ladies remained standing while their sergeant was speaking.

"These officers will be training on the tenth floor for the next few weeks along with officers Astor, Goodman, and Hill who will be starting in a couple of days. You will meet them at that time."

Rita looked at her husband-to-be, who was already looking at her smiling. This time, instead of shaking his head in disbelief, he nodded his head, showing his approval. She had to smile back.

"Thank you, Sgt. Ragland," as Lt. Williams chimed in.

"Remember when each of you are on your respective floors, you have no friends up there except your fellow officers. The people locked in the cells are criminals. They are there for a reason. You are not there friends. You are their jailer."

These are the very words Sgt. Ragland had told them the day before. It was evident these words were meant mostly for the new officers without uniforms. With that said, the lieutenant began calling out the floor assignments so the officers would know what floor to go to. It was no surprise that all of the new officers had been assigned to work on the tenth floor. So when the name calling had stopped, all of the officers headed to the elevator to begin the first of many rides to the tenth floor.

Training, Training, and More Training but What Were the Officers Learning?

CHAPTER 15

*W*hen the ladies arrived on the floor, their fellow officers were anxiously awaiting to be relieved of their duties, keys, and whatever headaches they had experienced that evening. The ladies met some new faces that they had never seen before, and they were all welcomed with smiles and handshakes.

"Give your keys to Edwards and Ogilvie for now. We will switch out as the night proceeds," said Sgt. Ragland.

The evening officers told the sergeant about all of the happenings of their shift that day, which included explaining their remarks in the 'pass-on book' and they quickly said their good byes. Sgt. Ragland knew the first question from her new recruits so she quickly answered their unspoken question.

"Ladies this is what we call the 'pass-on book.' Every floor has one in the control center, and everything that happens on a shift is written in the 'pass-on book' so all officers have documentation on incidents that transpired. This book is also so you have a record in case we need information for court purposes. So everyone will need to read the comments when you get to the floor and see how the entries are made because you will be writing in this book."

The first night for these new officers was filled with many memorable moments. First, there was learning the catwalk and how this particular walk had to be completed every hour to keep a watchful eye on the female inmates from the backside of their cells. Second, there was seeing how the inmates ingeniously learned how to communicate with the male inmates on the upper floors by way of the toilets. Then there were the exploits of Rosa Lynn. On the previous shift, she had set fire to her mattress yet again and flooded her cell. All of this information was noted in the 'pass-on book' as well as the time food was served, medications dispensed, and when inmates were pulled for classes or to see Chaplain Sizemore.

While all of the activities on a shift were basically the same, inmate classes and visits to see the chaplain were only completed during the morning and evening shifts. But without fail, each and every shift there were some incidents that happened involving inmates such as fights, illnesses, or out-of-the-ordinary catastrophes. This was day one of the many training sessions for the new officers on ten. But these were just the incidents with the inmates. What about the incidents with the officers not written for review in the "pass on book"? They really happened, and they must be told.

CHAPTER 16

*W*ell, days had turned into weeks, and weeks had turned into six months, and much had happened to the seven new officers working on the tenth floor of the Dearman County Sheriff's Department. Because of the rotation schedule every month, the seven officers had all worked with each other under the tutelage of Sgt. Ragland. Not only had they learned about jail life from the best trainer, they had all become fast friends. They were more like sisters than coworkers. It was safe to say that their friendship and mentor had made the best of what could have been a difficult work experience, given the conditions and type of work. What has transpired here was a new way of accepting a work assignment that was less than desirable.

"Last night we had a bus load of female prisoners transported here and they are all in holding cells waiting for shift change to be sent to the tenth floor. I am sending seven officers to assist

Sgt. Ragland with the overflow number of inmates," Lt. Whetson explained. Just as the officers change shifts every six weeks, so did the lieutenants in charge of each shift. As the lieutenant was beginning to call off floor assignments, the seven friends all looked at each other hoping they would all be assigned to the tenth floor.

"Astor, Edwards, Goodman, Hill, Ogilvie, Simmons, and Woodson—ten."

They all had small smiles on their faces not wanting any other officers to know their happiness at this assignment. Lt. Whetson finished his floor assignment call, and all of the officers began their upward assent up to their respective floors.

All of the officers who could piled into the elevator to go to their assigned floors.

"Why do you have that smile on your face?" Astor whispered to Officer Simmons.

"I will tell you when we get to the floor." A larger smile appeared on her face.

"What is it?" Astor asked again. Still no response from Simmons.

As the elevator came to a slow stop on the tenth floor, the eight officers descended to the control center. They were briefed by the officers they were relieving, and no sooner than Sgt. Ragland was engaged in looking at the 'pass-on book' and getting all of the needed information from the previous shift officers, Astor began her inquisition of her friend Simmons again.

"Why are you smiling?'

At this moment, Officer Simmons said no words but elevated her left hand to show the new diamond ring sitting on her fourth finger. Astor called her fellow officers to see Simmons's new engagement ring and get an explanation of what had transpired in the last day.

"Well, you know Deputy Bailey and I have been dating for almost six months. What you didn't know was when we first met I heard a bell and knew he was the one. But he thought I was a prisoner when he first saw me. After we got through that awkward moment, we got to know each other, and we honestly fell in love. Last week we went to the mall and looked at rings and this suede dress that was really expensive, but he said nothing.

Two days later, I was asleep and he called me and out of the clear blue he asked me if I preferred the dress or the ring. My eyes popped open, and I immediately asked him what he meant. He said he knew that I liked the dress a lot so it was my choice—the dress or the ring. I realized it was his way of proposing so, you know, I picked the ring. We went to the jewelry store last night."

Everyone was excited to hear the engagement news for Simmons. It appeared this was the time for love at the county jail. Within the last two months, Ogilvie and two officers from other shifts had become engaged in addition to Officer Hill. This had all of the signs of bridal showers but in actuality an opportunity to get together and party.

At this moment there was a loud noise coming from one of the nearby single cells. Reality set in, and the officers sprang into action. Three officers went to see where the noise was coming from while Sgt. Ragland and the other officers were taking care of the influx of new inmates now coming to the floor.

"Astor, you and Goodman go to the single cell area now and see what that commotion is and report back to me before you go to all of the cells and do a head count and see where each new inmate can go. Communicate this information back to me as soon as possible so I know what I need to do. Simmons and Edwards, work the picket area for now and make sure to document all information. Hill, you and Ogilvie go to shakedown and make sure there is ample clothing and clothing bags to put their street clothes in. If you see we need more supplies, call the other floors to get what we need here. Woodson, you will go with Miss Nurse as she gives out medication and evaluates the new inmates with medical issues."

About this time, Astor and Goodman returned from the single cell investigation. "The two inmates in the single cells have flooded their toilets and toilet debris is everywhere," reported Goodman.

Without batting an eye, Sgt. Ragland spoke her directives very succinctly.

"Simmons, call Lt. Whetson and tell him we need two trustees up here to clean the two cells and Astor move one inmate in the shakedown room while the trustees clean one cell and after one cell is cleaned, move the other inmate to the shakedown room.

Remember to stay with the trustees at all times so while you are transporting inmates, make sure the trustees are not left alone with either inmate. Let them stand near the picket while you pull each inmate. If the new inmates get here before the cells are cleaned, move the inmate from shakedown to the telephone booth, but make sure that the phone is disconnected if they have to go in there." Sgt. Ragland's directives were indeed delivered with no questions asked from anyone. At this moment, the elevator doors opened, and two male trustees with a male officer as their guide walked out with mops, buckets, and cleaning supplies.

"Follow me to the cells that need cleaning," said Sgt. Ragland.

While the sergeant was showing the trustees what needed to be cleaned, her officers were preforming their assigned tasks.

CHAPTER 17

No sooner had the trustees finished cleaning both cells than the eighteen new inmates began arriving on the floor. As they had been trained, the officers knew what to do and when to do it.

"Ladies, I am Officer Hill. The first five ladies, follow me into the shakedown room, and the rest of you follow Officer Ogilvie, who will show you where to sit until you are called."

The inmates followed instructions, and Sgt. Ragland's teachings were taking action as her officers were acting out their teachings. Miss Nurse arrived on the floor, and Officer Woodson greeted her as she got off of the elevator and escorted her to the cells where she dispensed medications.

"Hi, Miss Nurse," spoke Simmons.

"I have looked at the new inmates files, and it seems that five of them are taking some sort of medication. I have their files here for you to review."

58

"Thank you Simmons. Woodson, let me look at their files now before we do rounds. When they are assigned to a cell, let me know where they are so I can see them before I leave the floor today."

The first five inmates had been dressed out in their orange jail jumpsuits and escorted to their new living quarters. The second set of five inmates was taken to the shakedown area. Everything was working out just as Sgt. Ragland had directed when there was some commotion heard in the shakedown room.

"Goodman, come and watch these inmates so I can go and see if Hill needs my help," Ogilvie commented.

With no second thoughts, Goodman came to her fellow officer's assistance. As Ogilvie entered the shakedown room, she heard Hill speak the words, "If you ever attempt to hit me or any other officer on this floor again, you will need a body bag when I'm through with you. Do you understand what I just said?" asked Hill.

"Yeah, I hear you," the inmate responded.

"I didn't ask you if you heard me, I asked you if you understood. I will ask one more time. Do you understand me?"

"Yes, I understand you," the inmate said with a slight edge in her response.

"You really do not know who you are messing with, sister," commented Officer Hill. "You only get one chance to mess up, and this was your one and only time."

With that the inmate was more compliant from that moment on, and all of the inmates on ten quickly found out Officer Hill was no pushover.

She made sure to communicate to Sgt. Ragland what happened in the shakedown room, and per her instructions, this incident was written in the 'pass-on book.' Just as the sergeant had told her officers upon their first meeting, "You are not here to make friends with these inmates. You are here to make sure they know you are in charge. They will test you repeatedly, but you always be consistent with your words and with your actions. But never do anything that will cause you to be in one of these cells with them."

So, the first lesson that the ladies had been taught from their sergeant had been executed.

CHAPTER 18

The ladies worked expeditiously this night to make sure all new inmates were processed quickly. Sgt. Ragland made sure that all of her officers got an opportunity to work in the picket and the shakedown room until all inmates had been placed in a cell.

"Ladies, this was truly a well-oiled machine tonight," commented Miss Nurse. "I don't think I have witnessed such professionalism and comradery as I did during this shift. I will make sure to note these comments in my report to the lieutenant at the end of the shift. I can honestly say that you seven officers under the leadership of Sgt. Ragland work together well, and this is not the first time I have noticed it. Good job."

The officers all thanked Miss Nurse for her glowing comments. Sgt. Ragland chimed in with these same sentiments and praised each one of them for a job well done. It had already been decided that after their shift ended, they would indeed go to one of their usual hangouts to unwind from a hard but fulfilling night's work.

"Hi, officers. Good to see you again. Would you like the same booth?" asked Dorothy, the waitress at Lucas D&D. This small eating establishment had become a favorite place for the off-duty officers and friends to come and get good breakfast food and share horror stories about their job. The owner of this quaint restaurant, Lucas, had been at this Oak Lawn location for almost thirty years and when his wife died a few years ago, he and daughter Dorothy and son Darren, made a name for themselves when word of their famous pork chops made its way to the Deerman County Jail. Officers from various shifts were always at the restaurant since it was open twenty-four hours.

So of course Dorothy already knew that without menus, the officers would order the pork chop breakfasts that came with smothered potatoes and onions and soft scrambled eggs. This was indeed the breakfast after a hard but fulfilling night's work. For approximately two hours, the friends sat, talked, laughed, and ate their tiredness away.

"Tonight was a good night you guys," said Astor. "I know it was a good night because I didn't have one diet Dr. Pepper." About this time, Dorothy was bringing Astor her third diet Dr. Pepper, and all of the ladies chuckled out loud.

"So let's talk about men," said Woodson. Everyone looked at her with looks of disbelief.

"What are you talking about, Woodson?" asked Edwards. "Did you want to speak about a certain man topic or just men in general since you are married? We were just wondering."

"Oh, Lord," responded Woodson. I want to talk about all these engagements and upcoming nuptials. There's Hill, Ogilvie, and now Simmons. Is there something in the water?"

"Well," started Hill, "first of all, my wedding is in exactly three months. Your invitations should be in the mail in a couple of days. Second, it will be at the Fair Park Horticultural Center and it will be by invitation only so don't bring any uninvited guests. Third, you'd better be on time because if you're late, you will not be allowed to come in. Last, it will start on time." With these last statements, Hill took a long puff from her cigarette. End of her part of the discussion.

Ogilvie then began her part of this men conversation. "You all know Raymond and I are getting married but nothing as elaborate as Hill's wedding. It will be at the chapel on the NTU campus on Mockingbird Lane in about a month or so. There will be no invitations but you're all invited. I will give you the details later. Chaplain Sizemore from the jail will perform the ceremony, and I would like Simmons and Hill to stand with me. Don't get upset that you're not in the ceremony but the bride's maid's dresses I was able to purchase are for tall women. There will be no fanfare or after wedding celebrations because I have to go to work that night."

Simmons had to ask the question that was evident on everyone's face. "Why are you getting married on a day you have to go to work?"

"Because this is not a full-blown "love is a many splendored thing" type of wedding or marriage. He asked, and I said yes, mainly because he has a new washer and dryer that is really nice, so there—I said it. I love his washer and dryer more than him."

Everyone laughed out loud but they knew that Ogilvie was telling them the truth, and her mind was made up. "Okay Simmons, you're next," said Goodman. "Knowing you the way I do and the way you are grinning from ear to ear, this is a juicy tale. Let's have it."

"I already told you the story about the dress and the ring and how I had to make the final decision. Of course, I chose he ring. There are no dates, locations, or any plans yet, but I would love a summer wedding with my colors pink and green." "Those are good sorority colors," said Hill.

"I am sure my mother is already making phone calls and telling all of the family members, but Barry and I have not talked specifics about anything. One thing for sure—I want a big wedding. So all of you be prepared to be bridesmaids."

The officers who were first and foremost friends talked for another couple of hours before leaving to rest for their next night at Deerman County.

CHAPTER 19

$\mathcal{A}$s time slowly progressed, the ladies were tested and tested, and tested again, by Sgt. Ragland. These tests included county-approved, inmate-related tests and Sgt. Ragland's impromptu tests to make sure her officers knew each other in and out.

"Goodman, I need you and Astor to go to Parkland Hospital and sit with two inmates: Margo Meadowstone has to have some x-rays completed, and Rosa Lynn is having a procedure done. We made sure they had appointments on the same day, so we need two officers to accompany them. You can decide who watches whom, but remember: they are inmates," is all that Sgt. Ragland said to them.

When the jail van pulled away from the sally port at 6:30 A.M., the two most famous inmates on the tenth floor (one because she was a murderer and one because she was crazy enough to murder) left with two officers, who had been off of probation a few weeks.

"Officer Astor, I am so glad you and Officer Goodman are the ones looking after us today at the hospital," Margo Meadowstone said. "I agrees with what Grandma Meadows says," Rosa Lynn chimed in. The officers had no idea that this test had started at the sally port. The van pulled into the emergency bay at the hospital, and staff was waiting at the entrance to escort the handcuffed inmates into the hospital.

Margo Meadowstone had started her wounded-inmate conversation and look to gain sympathy from the staff, and anyone who would listen to her. The officers had decided that Goodman would stay with Margo and Astor with Rosa Lynn. What the inmates didn't know was that the two officers had already decided they would take their sergeant's words to heart and be on high alert. They already knew that both inmates, in their own ways, would try to escape and pull any tricks they could to make sure that happened. Both inmates had family in the city, so extra precautions had to be taken on this trip to the hospital.

"Hello, I am Dr. Bell and I will be running some tests on you today, Miss Meadowstone. There will be about four tests run today so we can see what steps we need to take."

"Hello doctor. I really do not feel well today; my joints are hurting, and these handcuffs are making the pain much worse."

"I understand," replied Dr. Bell. "We are going to take care of those pains today after we get the tests done. Orderly, will you please take Margo to the testing area?" The orderly did not waste any time doing what he was asked. "Sir, please let me make sure that Miss Meadowstone is ready to be transported," Goodman commented. She then strapped Margo onto the gurney, in addition to the handcuffs on her wrists. "Officer Goodman, I told the doctor that these handcuffs are making my joint pain worse. He said that they could be taken off while I was in the hospital, Margo stated."

"I understand, Margo, and we will take good care of you." With that, Margo was strapped to the gurney and pushed through a door that she had not entered. Not sure what was happening, she had to ask, "Where are we going? I thought we were going to the third floor for x-rays." Margo kept asking the same questions over and over, and no response from anyone was forthcoming.

After going through five different doors and up five floors on the elevator, Margo was brought to her final destination. "This is not where I'm supposed to be. Nobody knows I'm here," she kept repeating over and over. Goodman did not respond to her questions or concerns, nor did the doctor. What the two inmates did not realize was that the two officers had already spoken to the hospital staff and made arrangements for them to be isolated from the rest of the hospital population. Rosa Lynn was being held and watched in an isolated waiting room where no other patients were allowed.

"Okay Margo, we can now remove your handcuffs but we have to put restraints on your ankles while you have your tests," Goodman told her. So while her handcuffs were now removed, her body was restrained to the gurney, and her ankles were restrained as a second precaution. Margo was not happy at these changes she was not privy to, so she was relatively quiet.

As Margo was receiving her tests, Rosa Lynn was being watched by Astor. "Miss Astor, officer ma'am, I really has to go to the 'lil girls' room. You knows I got weak kidneys so I's really got to go." Officer Astor had no intentions of allowing her to go to the restroom so one of the nurses brought her a bed pan to use. When Rosa Lynn saw that she was not going to the restroom, she became violent.

"You is gonna regrets treating me this way. I told you I's had bad kidneys and I ain't using no pan to pee. Take me to the 'lil girls' room now. I's gonna git you fired when we get back to the jail."

"You either use this bed pan or use it on yourself," responded Astor in a calm voice. Rosa Lynn relented and used the bed pan, but Astor was also aware that she on many occasions had used her body waste matter as a weapon. "You use that bed pan and if you try anything you will have to be admitted to the hospital in a solitary ward. Believe me." She heeded Astor's words and used the bed pan without any fanfare. Noticeably upset and outdone, Rosa Lynn became quiet and had no further words to anyone.

When Margo's tests were completed, the inmates switched places and Rosa Lynn was taken to the same floor where Margo was for her procedure. The officers stayed with their respective criminals, and when both were finished and ready to go back go to the tenth floor, they were escorted out of the hospital from a different location than they arrived.

"Where is we going? I demand to know where you is taking us," questioned Rosa Lynn. "This is not the way we came in to the hospital," Margo chimed in. "Nobody can find us," she kept stating.

At this point, the officers knew that they had made the right decision to leave the hospital from a different entrance. They were sure that both inmates had planned for their family members to meet them there and probably try to help them escape. *Sgt. Ragland would be proud of us today, both officers thought on their way back to the jail.* So it was evident from this hospital outing today that these officers had learned their lesson well: inmates are criminals, no matter the situation.

CHAPTER 20

While the jail lessons were ongoing each and every day, there was one other training that the county required of their officers after their probationary period was over—the academy. Yes, our fledglings had come to the point in their training that would make it legal for them to carry a gun. Sgt. Ragland had done her part in preparing the officers for every possible jail scenario, and all of the ladies had learned their lessons well. Security was always uppermost in their minds on and off the job. The prisoners had come to know each officer not only by name but also by what they could get by with—nothing. All attempts by inmates failed, whether it was trying to escape, acquiring confiscated items such as drugs or weapons, or acting out in various ways. The officers handled all of these issues with successful outcomes. So this next and last chapter in their training was about to begin. This training would be like no other training they had experienced thus far.

The academy was composed of intense eight-week sessions that involved classroom and physical field exercises. Not only were these sessions intense, they were scheduled to test the mental and physical endurance of all officers. It was safe to say that the powers that be saw the need to make sure that all of the officers could handle the anguish and mind games that prisoners are known to try at every opportunity such as the constant inmate fights or attempts to injure officers with homemade weapons. As the seven friends had started this journey to become Deerman County Deputy Sheriffs, they were all assigned to attend the academy at one time. This was odd, but Sgt. Ragland added her explanation to the officers.

"The county usually does not send this many officers from one shift to the academy at the same time, but I have been told that you group of officers have caught the eye of the sheriff, and he wants you all trained together at the same time. The lieutenant has already rearranged many schedules to ensure the tenth floor is fully staffed while you are gone. Ladies, I am so proud of each of you. I can honestly say that out of all of the officers I have trained, you seven ladies have jelled the fastest and learned your lessons well. I am so proud of you. Go to the academy and make me even prouder. Oh, one other thing; Hill, since you have already been to the academy with your previous assignment, you will only need to attend the first six week sessions. After that, you will return to the jail on the midnight shift. You all are to report to the academy at the Decker facility on Monday morning at 7:00 A.M. for the first two weeks, and you will receive instructions at the end of this training. You will still come to work on the day shift one last time, and you will be off until Monday morning. Any questions anyone?"

"Sgt. Ragland if it is alright with you and the lieutenant, I would prefer to attend the entire eight-week sessions so I can make sure I know what my fellow officers are taught. It will still be a learning experience for me," replied Officer Hill.

"Hill, I think that is admirable, and I approve. I will speak to Lt. Whetson," commented their sergeant.

All of the officers had small smiles on their faces happy that they were still going to be training together. Sgt. Ragland took her leave from her officers and the minute she was out of sight, Astor commented, "Where are we going to celebrate tonight?"

"What about that club on San Jacinto? It's fairly new but I hear it has good entertainment, if you know what I mean."

"Oh, Lord, replied Woodson. I am going to have to tell Brian that we have a late meeting at work or something to get ready to go to the academy. I will think of something."

Everyone laughed at Woodson's comment. "Just so you know the club doesn't open until 10:00 P.M. so we need to get there about 10:30 P.M.," explained Astor. All of the ladies were excited at the thought of having a good time together again.

CHAPTER 21

*T*he ladies knew that they had to be at work early the next morning, but the club was calling their names. Just as she said earlier, Woodson, told her husband that she was meeting with her fellow officers to get ready for the academy. "Brian, don't wait up for me because we will be talking about our assignments at the academy and how we will complete them," she told him. He didn't know enough to ask why they needed to meet before they went to the academy and what lessons they would know beforehand. Goodman had to chime in with her own explanation news to her husband. "Forget all of that made-up stuff. I told my husband I was going to get drunk and I would be late if I came home at all. He just looked at me as I walked out of the door. I knew I was going to be drinking a lot, so I drove to Edwards so we could ride together. Edwards, where did you tell Evan you were going?"

"I said nothing to him. I told Monica I was going out with some friends, but she was already in bed. We have come to a mutual agreement that we will stay together until the end of the school year, so basically we are living two separate lives," Edwards explained.

So with that, they all met at *The Wellington* at 10:45 P.M. dressed in their club attire. Ready not to think about what they had done at work that day or even what they would be doing in a few hours, the ladies and officers were incognito and having a great time drinking, dancing, and doing whatever the moment warranted.

There was nonstop dancing and drinking by all, with Hill and Ogilvie drinking less than the others and designating themselves the appointed drivers in case there was the inability of some to drive on their own. "Ya'll, its 3 o'clock. We need to go home. We have to be at work in three hours," explained Woodson. Her fellow officers reluctantly agreed and began their slow walk to the entrance. As the ladies made their ways to their respective cars, it was evident that Goodman indeed needed driving assistance.

"I'm glad you had the sense to leave your car at my house," Edwards told Goodman. She would be spending the night with her friend.

All of the other ladies were able to drive on their own but with great care and attention to their driving habits. They all made it to their respective homes with the knowledge they would see each other again in less than three hours. Careful not to wake her husband and children as she entered her home, the first thing Woodson did when she arrived home was to brush her teeth and take a quiet shower to help erase the smell of the club from her body. Successful in her attempts thus far, she made her way to the bedroom and was about to climb into bed when Brian awakened and looked at the clock, which registered 4:30 A.M.

"You up already to go to work," he asked his wife. Thinking quickly in her somewhat drunken state, she responded. "Yes, I just thought I would get up early and fix everyone a good breakfast before I go to work." With that Woodson pulled off the night gown she had just slipped over her head and began putting on her uniform as she did every day before she goes to work. *I can't believe that Brian didn't even know I had never been to bed*, she thought. True to her word, she cooked her family a good breakfast and then left to go to work with no sleep.

As she arrived at the county to do another day's work, she made her way to the tenth floor, hoping she could get some sleep in the shakedown room before her shift started. When she got to the picket/control center to explain her intentions to the midnight shift, someone caught her eye. Ogilvie was already there in the space under the picket control center cabinet sound asleep with a pillow she had taken from one of the hospital beds.

"Ogilvie, what are you doing here?" she inquired.

"Woodson, I couldn't sleep at home so I came up here to rest and sleep before work. Why are you here?"

"Brian woke up as I was getting into bed, so I had to pretend I was just getting up and dressing for work. I came in to try and get about an hour or so sleep before our shift started."

"Grab a pillow out of the hospital and try to get at least an hour before shift change," commented Ogilvie.

The two ladies did indeed get some sleep in the very place where they spent a great deal of their time and where they are learning to become good officers. Not letting the night before deter them from their work duties, all of the remaining officers arrived for their shifts bright eyed with a little help from aspirin to do another day's work. Were these dedicated officers or what?

As hoped, all of the officers were assigned to work on the tenth floor their last day for eight weeks. Not showing any signs of her officer's sleep deprivation, their leader greeted them as they made their way to the floor. "Good morning ladies. This will be the last day you will be on the tenth floor for a few weeks. I am so proud of each of you and the progress you have made in your first six months. I have received more compliments on each of you from the lieutenant and even the sheriff. I can't tell you how happy that makes me. Now as we begin this next shift, I want to do an overall inspection of each cell and remove any contraband. The inmates hate these inspections so be prepared to get a lot of pushback.

The first one we will tackle will be Rosa Lynn. Simmons, you and Ogilvie move her to the phone booth and let her make a phone call while the rest of us clean her cell. She will not give you any trouble. It will take us about thirty minutes to give it a thorough cleaning. From there we will move to the single cells and then the hospital. We will leave the big cell areas to the end.

No one is expecting this inspection and it is early so we should not have too much grumbling." The ladies were in awe of how their sergeant had this inspection planned down to the second. "Okay it is now 8:00 A.M. and the inmates have just finished their breakfasts so let's begin our day and let's be thorough and be finished before lunch is delivered at 11:30. Any questions?" None of the officers had questions and with their silence, their day began.

Just as Sgt. Ragland, had explained, at 11:30 on the dot, the trustees bringing the inmate lunches were pushing trays from the elevators. All of the cells had been inspected and to the amazement of each officer, they confiscated ten homemade knives, seven spoons, and three drug paraphernalia items. The inmates were none too happy about losing their prize positions, but in the interest of officer safety, the tenth floor was again relatively safe.

Sgt. Ragland then showed the officers how to log and write up the paperwork to document their finds for the morning. "Boy, that was exciting," Woodson explained. All of her fellow officers were also pleased at the mornings work. What a way to begin their new journey.

FINAL EXAM TIME

What If I Have to Shoot Someone?

CHAPTER 22

So much has happened since our fellow officers met in October 1976, and there were many on the job lessons that have been learned. But as the lessons keep happening each and every day in the jail, the final test is yet to come: *what if I have to shoot someone?*

According to county rules and regulations, it was now time for the officers to attend the eight-week academy to learn the ins and outs of carrying a gun but most importantly, when you are obliged to pull your fire arm or even take a shot at someone. It seemed overwhelming to the ladies, but they were all looking forward to the new lessons they were about to embark upon.

"Good morning officers. Welcome to the 57th Deerman County Detention Officers Academy. I am Sgt. Whitstone, and I will be your supervisor for the next eight weeks." The ladies looked at each other each thinking the same thing, *Sgt. Ragland is our supervisor.* Sgt. Whitstone was a tall lanky man who had a limp when he walked. His receding hairline was more noticeable because he tried to cover up his lack of hair on the top of his head with the few strands from the left and right of his head. He used his glasses to keep the hair in place from the side of his head.

"I know you are all thinking this will be an easy eight weeks away from the jail and you can rest and relax for eight weeks. Be aware, after this eight week experience you will either be begging me to leave or I will be asking you to leave because you can't cut it. For those few of you who will complete the full eight weeks, you will become better officers who can carry a firearm. There is so much more to law enforcement than carrying a gun. An officer should be knowledgeable about all aspects of criminal behavior. Who can tell me what is the most important tool for any police officer? "

There were approximately forty officers from various police departments in the metroplex in this academy class, an even number of men and women, and they were all contemplating the answer to this question. Sure of his answer, one of the male officer's blurted out, "It's his gun" with a smug look and grin on his face.

"What is your name sir and why would you say that?" Sgt. Whitstone asked.

"My name is Arthur Rufford and because if a man has his gun, he can handle all situations and all people."

"Well, Officer Rufford, I am sorry to burst your bubble but the answer to my question is a pad and pencil. As officers, you will always need to carry a pad and pencil so you can document incidents and any information that you may need to remember if

82

you ever have to go to court and testify. Another thing Officer Rufford, female officers make up a large number of officers in every police department. Remember that!" Sounds of *oooooo and ahhhhhs* resonated throughout the room. It was apparent Officer Rufford had certain opinions about female officers, but would his opinions be the same after this eight week academy?

"Officers, in these next eight weeks, you will learn information on various subjects and by performing several activities. Please take out your notebooks and write this information down."

Week 1—Texas State Law
    Penal Code
    Code of Criminal Procedures
Week 2—Forensic Science
    The Medical Examiner and Understanding an Autopsy
Week 3—Report Writing
    Spelling and Writing
Week 4—Court Decorum
    Public Speaking
    Telephone Etiquette
Week 5—Traffic Laws
    Proper Driving
Week 6—Self-Defense
    Getting in Shape and Defending Yourselves
Weeks 7–8—Real-Life Scenarios
    Tear Gas

Firearm Instruction

Assaulting the Building

Final Exams

"Let me just say that while these are how each week has been planned, things could change based on how well each of you grasp the information. Also, while week six self-defense lessons are comprised of methods you will learn to defend yourselves in the jail and on the streets, you will be expected to exercise such as running to increase your endurance each day. You will need to bring proper running attire including shoes."

"How many miles will we be running each day, Sarg? I already run every day so this will be a piece of cake for me," commented Rufford.

"Let's get something straight Mr. Rufford. You will address me as Sgt. Whitstone at all times. I hope the running that you do has prepared you enough for what you will experience here for eight weeks, but I truly doubt it." Again there were more *ooooos and ahhhhhs* from the rest of the class. There were no other comments from officer Rufford this time.

"Are there any more questions at this time?" asked Sgt. Whitstone. There were no questions.

"Very well, it is now lunch time. So you have one and a half hours to go to lunch and be back in your seats exactly at 1:30 P.M., no exceptions. After lunch we will see a film about our state laws regarding the penal code and code of criminal procedures. You may want to take notes because you will be tested on this information as well as on all lessons. If there are no other comments or questions, you are dismissed for lunch."

With that, all of the members in the class quickly left this room and did what their sergeant told them, gladly going to lunch.

CHAPTER 23

"What did you all think?" asked Simmons to her fellow six officers. "I don't know about that exercise part."

"I was fine about everything he said except the exercising and the autopsy," replied Astor.

"Yes, I was fine until he said autopsy," commented Ogilvie. I will ask if this is mandatory because I really do not want to see an autopsy."

"Oh, Lord. Do you think we can get out of the exercising as well?" inquired Woodson.

"I don't think we can get out of the exercising. You might not want to ask that question," Hill replied. "I think what we need to make sure we do is excel at every lesson they present us with. That will make us look good as well as make the Deerman County Sheriff's Department look good. But most importantly, we will make Sgt. Ragland look good.

"I agree with Hill," said Goodman.

All of the ladies were in agreement about officer's Hill comment. Even though they all had looks of discontent on their faces, they knew what they had to do. However, what the ladies didn't know was that there were some male forces already in place to make sure none of the female officers succeed. How would the Deerman Seven overcome this trial?

Everyone except Rufford returned from lunch promptly at the appointed time. There was no comment from the sergeant about his tardiness, but his facial expression said it all.

The sergeant began his instruction. "Let's watch a short video before we begin our discussion. After the fifteen minute video, Sgt. Whitstone began his conversation.

"For the rest of the day we will start our conversation on the Penal Code and the Code of Criminal Procedure. First, you must be aware that the Penal Code is a code of laws concerning crimes and offenses and the subsequent punishments for each crime. In addition, The Code of—"

"Sorry I'm late Sarg, but I lost track of time. There was a game on the television and I got involved in the game. Completely forgot to eat lunch so I had to order me a burger to go. Ate it in the car. Sorry, Sarg."

Sgt. Whitstone did not comment on Rufford's explanation. He simply looked at him in silence while his fellow classmates all had looks of disbelief on their faces.

"As I was saying," the sergeant continued, "the Code of Criminal Procedures are the rules of how the courts will process a criminal case. It establishes the protection for the constitutional rights of suspects and defendants. I know it's hard to believe, but criminals have to have protection in the eye of the law even after they commit heinous crimes. If we didn't have these rules in place can you imagine what this world would look like?"

The rest of the day continued with discussions on these topics as well as how these regulations affect the way each officer performs his or her jobs. Much dialogue was had by the entire class except Officer Rufford. He appeared bored and not interested in this particular lesson by the question he asked in the midst of the sergeant's lesson."

"What does this have to do with learning how to shoot my gun?" he asked.

Again the sergeant ignored his question and continued his lesson. As the day came to a close, Sgt. Whitstone asked if anyone had any questions, and when there were no hands raised, he commented, "Everyone go home and read chapters 1–5 in your books and reread your notes from today as well as information from the video because there will be a test in the morning. You should be happy because I usually give a test the first day." Everyone looked amazed especially, Rufford.

"By the way, if I did not tell you already, there will be a test each day so I can make sure you are grasping what is being taught.

These test scores will be a part of your overall final grade along with your field activities. If there are no further questions, you are dismissed. Please be prompt in the morning and every morning. If you come to class after the test has begun, you will not be allowed entrance and you will fail that particular test. If you have three failing grades you will be dismissed from the academy. See you tomorrow. Rufford, I need a word with you."

As the students left the class, everyone looked at Rufford with the same facial expressions that said, I *wouldn't want to be you right now.* "What do you think Sgt. Whitstone is saying to Rufford?" asked Simmons. "I don't know, but I will bet you that there will be no more outbursts in class, and he will never be late again," responded Hill.

CHAPTER 24

$\mathcal{A}$t 7:45 the following morning, all academy students were in their places with bright shiny faces, *maybe not all,* but they were in their respective places, including Rufford. While class did not officially begin until 8:00, everyone wanted to make sure they were there for the beginning of the test. There were no smiles in the room and, as the sergeant entered, there were still no smiles.

"Good morning," Sgt. Whitstone said. "I will begin by passing out the tests booklets and you will have exactly one hour to complete the test. There will be no talking of any kind, and if you finish before the hour, which I doubt, close your booklet and sit quietly." *I thought I just graduated from college a few months ago, Simmons thought.*

At the end of the hour, everyone had basically finished their test with the exception of Rufford. He was still on page two of a four-page test. "Your test scores will be posted on the outside of the door each morning listed by the last four of your social security numbers. Today we will continue our discussion on the penal code and how these regulations affected certain court cases that actually happened and made headlines. Before we begin our conversation today, I want to give you your homework.

"You are to go to the headlines and you can go as far back as ten or more years and be able to report on the case, the judgement, and final ruling and if you agree with the decision or not. If you do not agree, you will need to explain your reasoning and state how it should have turned out. You can select a partner and tomorrow during your pre-sentations, one will discuss what initially happened and the other will tell the outcome. This is a fairly simple assignment, so I do not want a drunk driving case but something that made the headlines several days in a row. If you wish, you can bring in handouts or sources to support your presentation. I will dismiss you early today so you will have time to research your case and your report."

Goodman looked at Simmons. This last statement from Sgt. Whitstone gave her an idea for a presentation to the class with Simmons. *Simmons would be a good partner because she is good with words, she thought.*

"Are there any questions? If not, you are dismissed. After a brief discussion among themselves, the ladies decided they wanted to do a joint presentation if the sergeant agreed and they wanted to be the first presentation. They received the approval from the sergeant and immediately huddled together after the class to decide what their case would be, who was going to do what, and who would start the presentation. It was decided that Goodman and Simmons would go first and the others would follow suit to show the rest of the class they were indeed serious about how this presentation would make Deerman County look good.

The next morning the ladies were the first ones in class. They had decided that their presentation would show the progression of the same headline case from beginning to end.

"I bet you no one else has thought about doing what we are doing," commented Hill.

"So what is the order again that we will do our presentations?" asked Astor. Goodman responded with the breakdown of the order.

"Well, Simmons and I will be first because we will introduce the crime. Next will be Ogilvie and Hill, who will discuss the solving of the crime. Astor and Woodson will discuss the trial portion, and Edwards will finish everything with the sentencing, where they are now information, and our thoughts about this case. Simmons did you bring the tape recorder?"

"Yes, I have it right here."

"The other props are in the back of the room under the table," Woodson chimed in. "I will make sure that Sgt. Whitstone knows that our presentations have to be completed in the order that we just discussed so everything flows," commented Goodman. At this moment, the sergeant came into the room, and the ladies began to set up.

CHAPTER 25

"Good morning. Today we will begin our presentations, and the Deerman county officers have asked to begin the presentations today. They have evidently taken their assignment seriously and would like to share their information with the class," Sgt. Whitstone explained. "Officer Goodman, the floor is yours." There were looks of contempt on the faces of the male officers and other female officers but especially Rufford.

Goodman did not waste any time making her way to the front of the room to begin her well-prepared assignment. "This morning my fellow officers and I will attempt to explain to you what happened in the case that was entitled, The Voice Message Murder. The case was given the name because of all of the evidence surrounding the sounds you will hear on this recording and also how the police were able to use these sounds to solve this strange case." At this moment, the attention of the class changed, mostly from Rufford. All of the officers, or jury members, were sitting attentively and anxiously awaiting the next words from Goodman.

"Let me begin by saying that this is not a case about your normal voice messages, but a very bizarre case about the belief that an individual could possibly have a relationship with another individual they really did not know that well. Even though this information was taken from a real case in Louisiana in 1960 and of course none of us were there, we wanted to make sure you felt as though you were there. With that explanation, I am going to turn the next part of our presentation over to Officer Simmons who will take you to the beginning of our story. But before she begins, I would like for you to hear something."

At this moment, silence fell in the small classroom. Goodman positioned the small tape recorder on the podium and made sure the volume was turned up to the highest level. She then hit the play button.

"*Ooooooo, Haaaaaaaaa, Ohhhhhhhh, Yesssssss,*" were the sounds repeated over and over with a great deal of added moaning. These sounds and moans were of a female which drew even more attention from the class. The class immediately recognized there were no spoken words per se on this recording but merely sounds.

"*Who is that?*" you could hear being whispered throughout the room. It was even evident that Sgt. Whitstone was totally captivated by the beginning of this presentation. After a few moments of listening to these unusual sounds, the recorder was turned off and Simmons began her presentation. Her first words made a person

94

feel they were in a courtroom and opening statements were starting. She had the attention of the full class as well as Sgt. Whitstone.

"Ladies and gentlemen, let me begin by saying that this case tells the story of a couple who were never a couple. Were they star-crossed lovers or were they merely acquaintances? I will let you be the judge and jury in what we call, The Voice Message Murder. This is the story of three people, Joshua Collins, twenty-eight, Christopher Davidson, thirty, and Christopher's grandmother, seventy-five. These three lives were intertwined even though they never were formally introduced to each other, but only one of these people played the bigger role. Don't take my word; you be the judge after you hear all of the evidence. In about ten minutes, Simmons had explained the beginnings of this tale and finished her explanation of what happened in the beginning of this case. Then part two of this case was laid out by officers Ogilvie and Hill. You could literally hear a pin drop.

CHAPTER 26

Ogilvie and Hill took their position at the front of the classroom and began the next segment of this presentation. "You have heard the crime and why it was called The Voice Message Murder. But what you don't know yet is how the police caught the murderer," Ogilvie began. "Officer Hill will pass around pictures of the victim and the lead detective as I begin to explain the next phase in this case. Let's go to the conversation that the detective, whose name was Logan Jones, was having with his investigative team after he found the recorded messages.

At this portion of the presentation, Hill turned on the recorder again and the class heard the same *Ooooooos, Haaaaaaaaas, Ohhhhhhhhs, and Yesssssssses* as they had heard the first time. After she turned off the recorder, there was a silence in the room that could only mean one thing: they had, without a doubt, captured the attention of the entire class.

It wasn't just the recording, it was the fact that the officers had done their homework and prepared a report to the class that was informative and showed their instructor that they did understand the ins and outs of the judicial system. Ogilvie and Hill explained in great detail how the suspect became the suspect and how the police brought him to justice; the last part of the presentation would detail the trial portion of this case. The trial portion of the presentation would be presented by officers Astor and Woodson.

Officer Astor began, "As you have heard, Mr. Joshua Collins was murdered in 1960 by Christopher Davidson, who he worked with at the Mercantile Bank. The surprising part of this case was that over six months when Joshua picked up the ringing phone at his house, he heard a woman making erotic sounds, or so he thought. Imagine his astonishment when he finally realized his female phone stalker was a man pretending to sound like a woman. Officer Woodson will now pass out pictures of the victim, Joshua Collins, and the suspect, Christopher Davidson. As you take a moment to ponder the faces of these two individuals, Officer Woodson will take you to the six-month trial that ensued after the arrest of Christopher Davidson.

Officer Woodson, though nervous, began her commentary. "Picture yourself front and center at this trial of the century. There are the jurors who all have astonished looks on their faces because none of them had ever heard a voice message such as this one. Next, picture Christopher Davidson's frail grandmother being called to the stand by the defense to testify on her grandson's behalf. Then picture Joshua Collins murdered simply because he thought a woman was interested in him."

Woodson laid out the case to a tee, and the class felt as though they were front and center of this trial. After she laid out all of the information presented at this trial, it was time for Officer Edwards to give the closing statements and the final words from the jurors.

"Yes, your honor," is what the juror foreman told the judge when asked had they reached a verdict, started Edwards. "It took the jury two days to deliberate on this case and to come up with a final verdict for Christopher Davidson. What stumped the jury, according to the jury foreman, was the tape. They could not believe that this was indeed a man who sounded like a woman and murdered an unsuspecting man who just wanted some female companionship. After they got by this realization, they all agreed that Mr. Christopher Davidson was guilty. Their recommendation was for life without the possibility of parole. None of them even considered the death penalty as punishment even though Louisiana had this option available.

So the judge did act on their recommendation and sentenced Christopher Davidson to life without the possibility of parole on February 22, 1961. Mr. Davidson died on November 4, 1987, at the age of sixty from a heart attack. His grandmother died on March 22, 1961, one month after her grandson was sentenced. She, too, died of a heart attack, but her heart attack was broken at the loss of her grandson. One additional twist to this case that was buried deep in the small print of the last article about this case; supposedly his grandmother found four letters her grandson Christopher had written to Joshua Collins but never mailed. All four of the letters basically, said the same thing.

"Joshua, I truly love you. I don't know how you feel about me but maybe one day I will get up the courage to say these words to you."

The letters were all signed the same, "I Will Always Be Yours, Christopher."

This bit of information was never really highlighted more than a small paragraph in the newspapers. I guess you could say this was the second twist in this case. As we were researching this case and how it was solved and highlighted in the press, we feel the sentence was appropriate for the crime. However, while this was truly a sad case from beginning to end, the one person we all felt the sorriest for was Christopher's grandmother."

With this last statement, officer Edwards took her seat and there was total silence in this classroom. Sgt. Whitstone slowly stood from the back of the room and took his place in the front of the room. While much information was given by the Deerman County officers, their total presentations took exactly twenty minutes.

"Well," the sergeant began, this is definitely more than I expected. This presentation provided all of the pertinent information to let the listener know what happened from beginning to end. Now I hope the rest of you took notes because this is exactly what I expect from the rest of you." After the sergeant said these words, distinct mumbling could be heard in the background. With that, the class was dismissed for lunch with several presentations scheduled after lunch.

CHAPTER 27

*I*t was safe to say that the officers from the Deerman County Sheriff's Department had made a good impression on Sgt. Whitstone. At lunch they all said that they couldn't wait to tell Sgt. Ragland how well they did in their first presentation. "I guess staying up all night to get ready paid off," commented Ogilvie. Everyone else chimed in with their agreement.

"We have to always remember that whatever we do and say while we're in the academy reflects on the county as well as Sgt. Ragland," continued Hill.

After lunch there were several more presentations, but it was easy to see that no one else put the time and effort into what they presented as the Deerman County officers. Though no actual words were spoken out loud by Sgt. Whitstone, his expressions said it all. So at the end of this week and all of the presentations, the sergeant set the stage for next week's activities so everyone could be prepared.

"On Monday we will be taken by bus to the medical examiner's lab so we can see an autopsy up close and personal. For those of you who have squeamish stomachs you will have the option of seeing the facility but not the actual autopsy. However, keep in mind you will be expected to see the body beforehand and you will hear the explanation of what will be done. This part is not optional. I need to know who will not be witnessing the actual autopsy so I will know how to divide the class." Four hands went up; one female and three male. The female was Officer Ogilvie. Her fellow officers did not seem surprised because they already knew of her decision.

"Very well. We will leave this building at 8:00 A.M., so do not be late. No excuses will be accepted," as he looked at officer Rufford. No comment was made. "I have moved the schedule of activities around some so Tuesday we will begin our physical fitness workouts that will be complete at the end of each day. These workouts will consist of running and weightlifting to build up your endurance in the event you ever have to chase down a prisoner. Get ready because these next few weeks will move very quickly so be prepared. Are there any questions?" No one raised their hands, and the class was dismissed.

True to his word the bus left the academy building at 8:00 on the dot. When the students arrived at the medical examiner's lab at Southwest Institute there was total silence. Not knowing what to expect, the officers got off the bus tentatively. Once inside the building the first thing the students saw was an old lady sitting in a chair. "Wonder is she here to see a dead relative," said Rufford.

"Be quiet Rufford. Can't you see she's sleep," responded one of the other officers. Everyone became very quiet so as not to wake her when the sergeant escorted them into the autopsy room. When they got into the room the first thing they noticed was the cold temperature and all of the equipment used to perform an autopsy.

No sooner than they had entered the room, a gurney was wheeled in with what looked like a body under a sheet on it. The instructor explained what exactly was going to happen during the autopsy and what they would see. At this moment, he pulled the sheet back and there was the old lady that had been sitting in the chair outside. All were surprised, especially Rufford, who fainted at that moment. Sgt. Whitstone did not look surprised but explained. "There will come a time when you will need to know what a dead body looks like. You cannot assume that someone is asleep or pretending to be asleep if you're ever called to a crime scene. This exercise was to test your eyesight. Not if you could see but if you could surmise what you are actually seeing."

Some of the lab assistants did not seem surprised but immediately tended to Rufford. When he came to, he was embarrassed and escorted out of the room with the other four officers as the autopsy was about to begin. They were going to be given a tour of the facility and see all of the different areas that comprise the medical examiners department.

CHAPTER 28

When the autopsy was completed, the officers were taken back to the academy. There was further discussion about the procedures to complete an autopsy and what everyone had learned from this trip. The conversation lasted until Sgt. Whitstone said these words, "I am changing the schedule again. Since we have some time left in class today I would like to begin our physical fitness activities. Everyone has fifteen minutes to meet me outside on the track. If you did not bring your workout clothes today, you will walk the track to get a feel for it but for those of you who did, change and you will begin by running one mile today. By the end of the academy you will be expected to run five miles," explained the sergeant. Astor had this strange look on her face, but she never said a word.

Sgt. Whitstone was on the track waiting for everyone in ten minutes. Slowly dragging to their destination, everyone was ready in fifteen minutes, all in their workout clothes.

"I will be the lap keeper so you will know when you have completed the entire mile." Astor had that strange look on her face again but she spoke no words. When the sergeant blew the whistle for them to begin everyone started reluctantly but soon all began their assigned task.

"This is not what I had in mind when I came to the academy. I am not cut out for this. There has to be a better way," Woodson stated.

"You can do it Woodson," said Simmons. "We will run together," she said. No sooner had they run to the back of the building on the first lap of the track, they noticed some movement in a set of bushes in front of them. As they got closer, they saw Astor hiding in the bushes.

"What are you doing, Astor?" Woodson asked.

"I do not like to run, and I will not run today. Just let me know when the sergeant has blown the whistle for the last lap and I will run then. This is not me," she replied.

"Aren't you afraid of getting caught?" asked Simmons.

"Maybe, but not if you help me. I cannot do this today."

Both of the ladies agreed and just as some of the other officers were approaching, they began running again. Who would have ever known that Astor was able to hide when she needed to hide and run only in those instances when it counted and this would last for three weeks until her fellow officers helped her on the weekends and after academy times? But as you could guess, Astor became an excellent runner outperforming many of the male officers. Deerman County Sheriff's Department comrades to the rescue again.

Needless to say that time at the academy flew by. All of the officers were becoming more proficient in every aspect of their training. The seven friends helped each other master certain lessons and exams so they would all be successful.

For example, Officer Simmons minored in English, so because report writing came easy to her, she helped her fellow classmates with this set of lessons; Edwards had a knack for the ins and outs of Court Decorum given her prior experiences and learning what departments were responsible for certain tasks; Hill was proficient in self-defense techniques, getting in shape, and handling firearms. She had learned how to properly defend herself and handle firearms in college when playing in various pool tournaments. She always won.

Goodman and Woodson equally excelled with mastering traffic laws. They laughed that because they had to drive children around all the time they had to be careful. It was so funny to them that after the first lesson on traffic safety that Edwards backed into a pole. "Hey how do you drive when you are driving, Monica?" they all teased and laughed at her. Finally, Ogilvie and Astor had little problems with the instruction on tear gas and assaulting the building. The male officers were amazed at how they were able to tolerate the tear gas with little or no affects and outperform them when entering a burning building. It was no wonder that these officers passed each exam with flying colors because they worked as a team to help each other. This was the first lesson they learned from Sgt. Ragland. She would be proud.

So at the end of the eight-week academy, all of the officers in Academy Class #57 graduated, and no one was left behind, not even Rufford. His lessons extended well beyond the academy lessons thanks to Sgt. Whitstone. While there were no special commendations for any of the officers who attended the academy and who did exceptionally well, Sgt. Ragland did receive a personal letter from Sgt. Whitstone about her seven officers.

Sergeant Ragland
Tenth Floor Training Officer
Deerman County Sheriff's Department
Deerman, Texas

Sergeant Winifred Ragland,

The Graduating Academy Class #57 has recently completed their eight-week course work and are now ready to assume their respective duties at the Deerman County Sheriff's Department. While it is not a practice of the Academy to award commendations to individual officers, I have the authority as their training officer during this period to inform the supervisor as I see fit of certain areas of proficient performance.

The seven officers that attended the Academy from Deerman County did indeed excel in all areas of coursework during the entire eight weeks. I saw a comradery and willingness to learn the material with each lesson they encountered. They worked together as a team and as a team received some of the highest test scores of any class from the same department and from any other law enforcement department. This can only be attributed to the training and instruction they have received thus far under your tutelage.

It has been my pleasure getting to know these officers and to have been their Academy instructor. Please ensure that each officer receives a copy of this letter and that a copy is placed in their employment file. Thank you, Sergeant Ragland for a job well done in preparing these officers to face life's challenges in and out of the jail.

Sincerely,

Sergeant Andrew Whitstone
Academy Instructor

When the officers returned back to their jobs at the sheriff's department, they had all been assigned to come to work that day and work on the tenth floor. They were ecstatic at returning and, believe it or not, seeing all of the inmates but especially Sgt. Ragland. Unaware of the letter from Sgt. Whitstone, the ladies stepped off of the elevator to see Sgt. Ragland standing in the picket with a big smile on her face. She was happy to see her officers.

As the officers approached the inside of the picket, they noticed a folder with each of their names of it and a big bowl of trail mix. Not sure what to make of this surprise, they each hugged Sgt. Ragland and waited for the explanation.

"Ladies, I am so very proud of you and all that you accomplished at the academy. I received a letter from Sgt. Whitstone about your performance during this period."

I wonder did he find out I didn't complete the laps every day and that Simmons and Woodson helped me, thought Astor. I know he's telling her about not viewing the autopsy, Ogilvie was thinking at the same moment. All of the officers were all thinking about things they did or didn't do that had finally caught up with them.

Sgt. Ragland handed each one their folder and asked that they read the contents. As they began to read, their facial expressions changed and they all seemed amazed. "Ladies I cannot tell you how happy this makes me. I asked the Lieutenant if you all could be assigned to work together today so I could tell each of you how proud I am. You all have indeed learned what I have tried to teach you these last few months. I made some trail mix to celebrate how well you did at the Academy. The lieutenant as well as other officers will be stopping by periodically to say job well done."

The ladies were speechless but smiling. They were so happy to be home.

Do You Take This Officer or Birthday Girl?

CHAPTER 28

*I*n the next few months the officers were indeed back home on the tenth floor of the Deerman County Sheriff's Department as well as in their personal lives. Hill, Ogilvie, and Simmons were all preparing for upcoming nuptials in various locations and formats. But county duties came first. According to county rules and regulations, when their officers have successfully graduated from the academy, they are considered fully trained in all jail procedures, which meant they worked on other floors in the jail with the men prisoners and on occasions escorted them to various locations such as court, hospital, and other incarceration facilities.

So given the county powers that be, no time passed until the seven officers' experience and training was put into action. Astor, Edwards, and Goodman were assigned to escort a serial murderer on the transport bus to the TDC (Texas Department of Corrections). The bus was scheduled to leave the jail sally port at 5:30 A.M. The sally port was the area where prisoners were taken to or from the jail in police vehicles, vans, or buses. The three officers were instructed to be at the sally port dock no later than 5:00 A.M. They had already been briefed on the prisoner's tendencies while in jail and his past crimes.

"Mad Dogg Brennan is considered very dangerous and cunning and has to be watched at all times. He is not to be trusted no matter what he says to you. Yes, Mad Dogg is his real name, and he lived up to it in every sense," the lieutenant said in the briefing to the three officers.

"Okay ladies, let's remember our academy and Sgt. Ragland training," Astor commented. "Let's always make sure that one of us is in front, one in back, and one on either side of this prisoner," she continued.

No sooner had they finalized their plan, Mad Dogg was being led out of the door in handcuffs by two male officers.

"Boy he looks like a real dog," Goodman whispered. They all made sure they looked at Mad Dogg straight in his eyes and that he saw them looking at him. As he was led closer to the bus Edwards noticed something was not right.

"If this prisoner is so dangerous, why doesn't he have leg irons on?" Edwards asked. She immediately went to the officers escorting him out and asked them that very question.

"Oh we put them on the bus so they wouldn't slow us down," one responded.

No sooner had these words left his lips when Mad Dogg tripped the officer on his left who fell over the sally port dock and was knocked unconscious after hitting his head on the concrete. In a split second the officer on the right was elbowed in his chest, and Mad Dogg took off running. Not even taking time to think it through, Edwards and Goodman took off running as well. Astor stayed behind and made sure that the two officers got medical treatment. Because Edwards always excelled at running long distances, Mad Dogg had nothing on her.

"Stop, stop, stop," Edwards kept yelling at Mad Dogg but to no avail. Goodman was slowly keeping up with the two. She had already called the county and told them where they were and you could hear the sirens in the background. Edwards was getting closer to Mad Dogg when he suddenly grabbed a woman who was standing at a bus stop and put her in a choke hold. At this point, Edwards caught up to him and the woman. She had pulled out her gun hoping she didn't have to use it.

"Let her go Mad Dogg, Let her go or I will shoot," Edwards kept repeating.

"If you don't back off and let me go I will break her neck," was his response.

"You know I can't do that. Let her go."

At this moment the woman started flailing her arms because she was being choked. Showing no remorse or stopping his efforts at escaping through his attempts at choking his hostage, Edwards made good on her promise. She shot Mad Dogg in the left leg and he immediately released his hold on the woman. Goodman stepped in to help the woman, and by this time a sheriff vehicle and ambulance had arrived. Needless to say, this was a day that was not expected by Astor, Edwards, or Goodman, but as usual, the officers had demonstrated their lessons well.

"At least we won't have to go to TDC now," Goodman said. The two smiled as they were driven back to the jail.

CHAPTER 30

It seemed that only a few days ago since the escape attempt with Mad Dogg and Officers Astor, Edwards, and Goodman but weeks had elapsed and wedding bells were ringing in the background. First, there was the wedding of Officer Hill on the horizon. By all accounts this was going to be an affair, *wedding*, of the year. Of course all of her seven jail comrades, including Sgt. Ragland, had been invited, and all were looking forward to attending. It was odd that for most occasions that the friends got together they were all off at the same time. No one questioned this fact; they were just happy it worked out that way most of time.

"We have to give Hill a bachelorette party. It doesn't have to be a large party but we have to celebrate somehow," Simmons commented.

A look of excitement came over Ogilvie's face. "Hey, I know what we can do. "There is an O'Jays and Whispers concert in Fort Worth, and we should go." I can rent a van and we have to make sure we invite Sgt. Ragland. I think she will enjoy that. Okay. Who's in so I can see if I can get tickets?"

No one ever looked at Sgt. Ragland as their supervisor outside of work. Because of their respect for her, they looked at her as one of the gang. Her age was never a consideration. However, when she was told of the upcoming plans, she explained that she would love to go but she had been called to work when one of the shift supervisors became ill. Everyone understood, and they knew this would not be the last time they would invite their sergeant to a night with the girls.

Because it was a bachelorette party, Hill's older sister, Barbara, was also invited. What a night it was going to be. They all agreed on the time and location to meet, and the party was on.

They had all arrived at the Fort Worth Convention Center at their designated spot.

"Ya'll I can't stay out as late as the last time we went out," Woodson explained. "I still can't believe how that worked out."

Everyone laughed and agreed with her. As the concert began, the party was on. The Whispers sang all of their hit songs in two hours and it was a wonderful concert so far. The songs that really got these ladies on their feet were the upbeat songs like *"Rock Steady"* and *"It's a Love Thang."* But the party was just beginning. The O'Jay's came on stage singing *"Ship Ahoy"* dressed the part in pirate costumes. Ogilvie was right. This was indeed a wonderful bachelorette party. They not only enjoyed the concert, they enjoyed being with each other. This was a night to remember.

"Let's go and grab some food at Lucas D&D. It's still early," said Woodson.

So topping the night off with a good meal with friends sealed the night. Many decisions were made over conversations at this particular restaurant, which had become known as their restaurant. Some of the most important decisions were decided on this night by these officers by day and party animals by night.

"Let's all wear hats to Hill's wedding," suggested Astor.

"Is that the alcohol talking? I don't even own a hat." responded Simmons.

"Neither do any of us but it's a good idea," Ogilvie agreed.

All Hill could do was laugh just thinking about them in hats at her wedding. But it was settled. Hats it was.

"One last thing before we leave here tonight. Do not, I repeat, do not be late to the ceremony or you won't get in, Woodson," commented Hill.

Everyone laughed at this statement, but Woodson was known for being late on several occasions. So all she could say was, "Oh Lord."

CHAPTER 31

The first of three wedding days had arrived. Officer Laura Hill was to become Mrs. Daniel Potter on this appointed day. She had received much advice on what to do and what not to do from her family and friends. While she appreciated hearing all of the sage advice she received from her married friends like Woodson, Edwards, and Goodman, the one piece of advice that gave her a laugh and something to remember was from Sgt. Ragland. One day when all of the ladies were assigned to work on the tenth floor Sgt. Ragland felt it was her duty to impart some sage advice to the couples preparing for their weddings: Hill, Ogilvie, and Simmons.

"While Hill, Ogilvie, and Simmons are all getting ready to get married, I would like to tell you all what I have found to be true about marriage. No matter what you do to keep your marriages a gift from the Lord each and every day, first and foremost, never let the love die. You have to poke the fire every now and then. You don't have to do what I did but you will have to do something.

"One Halloween night, it was a busy trick or treat night on our street. My husband always liked going to the door to give out the treats to the kids in the neighborhood. I got this idea that I knew he would love and always remember. I was going to be one of those trick or treaters."

The ladies all looked at each other with bewildered looks on their faces. Not sure where this conversation was headed, they all listened attentively.

"I got this idea of what my costume could be so I grabbed my husband's trench coat from the closet while he was handing out candy. I went into our bedroom and finished putting on my costume and snuck out the back door and went around the house to the front door. I waited until there were no children in sight coming to the door, and I walked up to the door and rang the bell. Zachery opened the door and I opened my trench coat and all I had on was my birthday suit. Zachery dropped the basket of candy and his mouth flew open. He was speechless. I have to say that was one of my better tricks. No sooner than I had closed the trench coat back up, my grandkids pulled up in the driveway."

Sgt. Ragland started laughing at her own story, and so did her officers. They could not believe their sergeant was telling them this story, but they all knew what message she was trying to tell them.

"My husband talked about that night for many years. He always wondered what I was going to do next. I had to keep the flame burning in my marriage and so do each of you. One day I will tell you about the trampoline." *They all thought the same thing: what about the trampoline?*

"Wow, that gives me a good idea," Woodson said.

"Woodson, if you do the trench coat, make sure your children are out of the house," Astor replied as the other ladies laughed.

Sgt. Ragland was always giving the ladies advice on marriage and what things a wife should always think about regarding keeping her husband happy. They always listened to her.

CHAPTER 32

The big day had finally arrived. Hill's wedding was taking place at the Horticultural Center at the Fair Park. It was a beautiful day and a perfect place for a wedding. The ladies decided to go together to the wedding so as not to be late and to have fewer cars. As planned, all of the ladies wore their hats. There was Astor in her white hat, Edwards in her green hat, Goodman in her pink hat, Ogilvie in her yellow hat, Simmons in her red hat, and Woodson in her black hat. There was an array of colors. Again, Sgt. Ragland could not make the ceremony due to work schedules but the ladies understood.

As Hill slowly walked down the aisle in her beautiful white satin wedding dress with the long train, she could see her friends sitting on the front row of the left section of the room. First she saw their hats and then their smiling faces. All she could do was smile more than she already was.

After the "I dos" were said and the kiss was completed, the party began. There were lots of people in attendance, lots of food to eat, and lots of music to dance to. Our hatted friends did it all.

One person that they met at this shindig was the mother of the bride who became not only the mother of the bride but someone they came to know as Miss Minnesota *(this name was a story in and of itself)* and visit on occasion. It was a good wedding day for Mrs. Laura Potter.

Now on to the second of these county weddings that took place three weeks after Potter's wedding; it was Ogilvie's turn. On a much smaller scale, Ogilvie had an intimate ceremony at a beautiful chapel on the SMU campus. She decided that there would be no certain colors in particular, and while her sisters and parents were in attendance, her chosen bridesmaids would be the new Mrs. Potter and Simmons. Because of the time that the ceremony was taking place, only Potter and Simmons were in attendance from the group. The minister performing the ceremony was none other than one of the county chaplain's, Chaplain Seikland. She had become a good friend to all of the officers and on occasion went out with them on one of their girls' night out, and she was happy to perform this ceremony. This was a beautiful ceremony as well with the bride wearing a simple V-necked cream-colored dress with a small hat. After about a twenty-minute ceremony, Joy Ogilvie became Mrs. Joy Grant.

The party continued at a small reception at the house of one of Joy's sisters. It was a small, tasteful, and intimate affair, and the bride was glowing. Her family got a chance to meet some of her jail family they had heard so much about. It, too, was a good wedding day for Mrs. Joy Grant.

The third county wedding had been scheduled to take place exactly one month after the new Mrs. Grant's wedding but due to some health issues for Simmons it was postponed for several months with no set date. However, the new wedding day for Simmons was also a small intimate affair and took place at her maternal grandmother's house in the living room. The bride wore a layered white wedding gown and carried a bouquet of white calla lilies. Because the date for the ceremony was decided in one day, none of her jail comrades could attend. But again, Chaplain Seikland performed the small ceremony, and Rita's family and some neighborhood friends were in attendance. A small reception followed the ceremony into the wee hours. This again was a good wedding day for Mrs. Rita Bradford.

CHAPTER 33

Things sort of went back to normal in the next few months. Even though three of the friends had gotten married, they still called each other by their maiden names. However, one day when the ladies were all assigned to work on the same day but on different floors, Ogilvie had some news that she wanted to share with her friends. After work they all decided to go to their favorite restaurant. Before she got into her news, they all decided to take Sgt. Ragland out to celebrate her seventieth birthday. So as they made these plans, everyone noticed that Ogilvie was quieter than normal.

"What is it, Ogilvie? I can see it on your face," asked Simmons. At this moment, the others saw the same thing and wondered what was going on.

"Roger has been transferred to Tennessee. We will be leaving in one month. He is there now looking for a house. I am not happy that I have to leave. I think if I had known this when we got married, I would have had second thoughts. But he had that washer and dryer that I couldn't pass up."

All of the ladies laughed as well as Joy. The rest of the day was dedicated to remembering the beginnings and what would continue even after her move to Tennessee.

The day of Sgt. Ragland's surprise birthday outing had arrived. Still not sure what the ladies had in mind, the sergeant was ready for her surprise. The ladies again rented a van and they all left from the county to parts known to everyone except their sergeant. Once they drove onto the parking lot of this establishment, a big smile came to Sgt. Ragland's face, and the officers knew they had made the right choice. As the ladies entered the establishment, the music was loud, and there were flashing lights everywhere.

"Good evening, ladies. Welcome to La' Bare. Do you have a reservation?" the hostess asked.

"Yes, it is a birthday celebration for Winifred Ragland," Edwards responded.

"Yes. I see it. Happy birthday to you ma'am. Follow me, please." The ladies followed the hostess to their table, which was front and center of the stage. The ladies wanted their friend to have a bird's eye view of everything on her special day and give her something to remember.

"You girls are so sweet for doing this for me," she responded. "I intend to have a good time and maybe even have one or two of those mixed drinks since I'm not driving."

Laughter filled the room at this comment, and the night was off to a good start. As the show began a group of ten men came onto the stage dressed scantily with muscles showing from every part of their bodies. The birthday girl was looking at each and every one of them in amazement. She could not believe how much fun she was having.

"My husband used to look like number four," she commented. The ladies were always amazed at some of the comments their sergeant said to them. She always counseled them on what makes a good marriage and how to make sure your husband stays happy. That's why it was a consensus amongst the ladies that this was the perfect place to bring their sergeant for her birthday. Because she was a woman of her word, Sgt. Ragland did indeed have two mixed drinks on her birthday. While everyone knew she was not a shy woman by any means, it was no surprise when the men came down from the stage and into the audience that the birthday girl got up from her seat and began dancing with the designated man at her table.

"Why does he have money in his underwear; it's my birthday not his? Am I supposed to give him some money too?" she asked.

"If you would like to, we have some money for you to give him, but you have to put it in his underwear."

"Oh I see. Give me about $10. He's doing a good job dancing."

Showing no fear, the ten-dollar bill was placed in the dancer's *underwear* and Sgt. Ragland finished her dance. Soon after she sat down, a birthday cake was brought to the table with many lit candles, and the entire room of people singing happy birthday to her. Everyone could see what a wonderful time she was having, and her officers were so happy they had given her this night. After about two hours, it was time to go. What a birthday to remember!

Do You Remember When?

CHAPTER 34

*I*t is so hard saying goodbye to friends who are like family to each other. But this is exactly what happened to the eight on ten family. Many years have passed and many changes have happened in the lives of each and every one of the longtime friends. First, Ogilvie has moved back to Texas without Roger and none of the remaining seven ladies work for Deerman County anymore. Everyone has gone their separate ways including Sgt. Ragland, who retired as a court bailiff. As with any biological family there have been divorces, marriages, births, deaths, and the occasional family reunion. So it is safe to say that there were family reunions for this group.

Unlike the unexpected good and bad things that they all experienced, the reunions were most always planned and implemented by Simmons. She became the social consultant of the group by her choice because she liked staying in contact with her jail family. Given that everyone lived all over the state, there was no hesitation to all gather in the locations close to their jail mother and mentor,

Sgt. Ragland. Though no longer their sergeant, she was simply Miss Ragland.

"Okay, Simmons, I got Miss Ragland's address from her daughter Sandra. She lives in Corsicana, Texas now at the Senior Autumn Assisted Living Facility," commented Edwards.

"We will be leaving Deerman at 9:00 A.M. and will meet you at the home at around 11:00 A.M. in time to have lunch with Miss Ragland," replied Simmons.

At 11:10 A.M. the six travelers pulled into the parking lot. Edwards was already there waiting on her friends. The ladies took another ten minutes to greet, hug, and briefly catch up with each other before going in.

"Okay I have already gone in and gotten Miss Ragland's room number. The front desk said we could go straight to her room. Sandra had already called them to let them know we were coming," explained Edwards.

With this explanation, they found their way to the designated door and gently knocked. There was a faint voice on the other side that said, "*Come in.*" As the door slowly opened, Miss Ragland was sitting on her bed, putting on her shoes, and getting ready for lunch in the dining room. Once she saw the seven ladies walk into her room a huge smile came over her face.

"I am so happy to see you girls," she commented. "Oh my, you girls look so good, and I am so happy you came to see me. This is a total surprise. How did you know I was here? What have you all been doing? My, you girls so do look good to me." Miss Ragland was so happy to see her friends that no one could answer one of her many questions. She hugged and kissed each one at least twice. After all of the hugs and kissing, they finally were able to explain to her that her daughter Sandra had helped them with their visit today.

"Lord, that girl. I love her for letting you all surprise me like this," she replied. "Can you girls stay a while?"

"Yes we are going to have lunch with you today," answered Astor.

So after more hugs and kisses, the eight from ten went to have lunch together.

CHAPTER 35

No one really ate too much lunch on this first of many visits to come. There was a lot of talking and laughing and hugging.

"Do you remember when we cooked catfish on the tenth floor after we got back from the academy?" asked Woodson. Laughter filled the room with this first "do you remember" moment.

"Yes," said Ogilvie. I don't even like fish, but I was the one who brought the fish."

"I brought the salad," chimed Goodman. "Yes, and I brought all of the cooking utensils," continued Hill. "How did we ever get all of that stuff up to the tenth floor?" asked Edwards.

Baffled by this revelation, Miss Ragland had to admit, "I don't remember that."

Everyone laughed again and the explanation of how this jail catfish cookout came to be was started by Simmons.

"It was a Sunday. All of us had been assigned to work on the tenth floor that night because there had been a lot of inmates transferred to the floor that week. We each brought a little at a time that whole week and hid everything in the small kitchen. That Sunday we brought the fish upstairs in a bag and everyone thought it was clothes. The fish was still a little frozen so it did not smell."

No one was eating lunch, especially Miss Ragland, because this was news to her. Astor continued the explanation after finishing her first diet Dr. Pepper.

"You know on Sunday's that St. Stephen's church comes to the jail and usually two of us have to accompany them to the cells to see the inmates. On this particular day, Miss Ragland and Hill were the escorts, As soon as you went into the cells, we began cooking. The inmates had just eaten, so even though they smelled the aroma, they never said a word to us. This was also the day that Hill decided to sing a song after the associate pastor gave his message. She sang 'Soon and Very Soon.'"

"I remember that part," said Miss Ragland. "What happened next?"

"What I remember was that while Hill was singing every verse of the song, I had enough time to get everything cooking," continued Woodson. "Simmons made the salad, and Ogilvie and Astor went on the catwalk to keep up appearances. Goodman and Edwards stayed in the picket in case someone got off of the elevator. By the time you all had been to every cell, and Hill sang her song, we had finished the preparing and cooking. When you all were finished with the church group, we had made plates for everyone—and even you, Miss Ragland. You just thought we had brought you a plate of catfish from home. So we explained the smell by saying we were heating the food up in the oven, and no one thought any different."

"Lord, you girls kept me on my toes and laughing all the time," Miss Ragland expressed. "I was never happier than when you girls came to work at the Deerman County Sheriff's Department."

"Miss Ragland, do you remember what happened when you finished eating your meal?" asked Edwards. "Woodson tried to tell a joke about a couple who had just gotten married, and she got the punch line wrong over and over again. You got so tickled that you almost peed in your pants."

"Lord, you girls always had me almost peeing in my pants," laughed Miss Ragland. "I remember the time Woodson and I was in the picket and you girls were in the tanks or on the catwalk. I was talking to Woodson about an entry in the 'pass-on book', and she was standing behind me. I asked her a question but she didn't answer. I asked her again and she still didn't answer."

"Oh Lord," said Woodson.

"I looked around and she was sound asleep standing up. I laughed so hard that time that I think I did pee in my pants." Everyone including Woodson enjoyed this long-forgotten story.

Ogilvie chimed in with a Miss Ragland story. "Miss Ragland, remember when you told about you surprising your husband one Halloween with the trench coat at the front door"?

"Yes," she answered. "Did you try that?"

"I did. When Roger and I moved to Tennessee, he had come home from a long day at work. He was tired, and I had a nice hot meal prepared for him when he got home. After we ate he went into to watch a little television. I thought about your advice, so I put on his trench coat and went out the back door and walked around to the front door and rang the doorbell. I rang it three times, and he never came to the door. The front door was locked so I had to walk back to the back door, and it had locked itself. I knocked and Roger never came to the door. Luckily I had left the kitchen window unlocked, and I had to climb in the window. I went into the living room and Roger was nowhere to be found. I went to the bedroom, and he was sound asleep on the bed. Needless to say I didn't try that again. I threw that trench coat away."

"That's not supposed to happen." Seriously, she later explained, "You have to do it when he is alert and awake."

Everyone laughed again. The laughter was getting louder and louder, and attracting the other residents in the dining room as they were joining in with their laughter as well.

CHAPTER 36

These semi-planned and on occasion impromptu mini-family reunions occurred at least twice a year now. Her daughter Sandra was always so grateful for the visits her mother received and the love shown to her. She never told her mother when she was going to have company because she knew she loved surprises.

Usually the ladies tried to see Miss Ragland at the beginning of summer and a time in between her birthday and Thanksgiving. These visits were planned so there was always a meal involved. On at least three occasions Miss Ragland was taken to the local Tex Mex restaurant because she liked eating cheese enchiladas.

In 2005 on one of the planned Thanksgiving dinner reunions, four of the seven ladies arrived right before lunch was being served in the dining room. As they had done on every visit, they went directly to Miss Ragland's room and they knocked on the door. A frail voice was heard saying, "Come in." The door was opened and the ladies saw their friend just sitting on her bed. She took one look at the ladies and smiled but unlike past visits, did not recognize them.

"Hello. Can I help you?" she asked.

"Hi Miss Ragland. It's Edwards, Ogilvie, Simmons, and Woodson. We came to have Thanksgiving lunch with you today."

"Lord, I don't remember your faces but I'm so glad you girls are here."

It was evident that Miss Ragland was not seeing or hearing as well as she had been in past visits. Also her memory was getting a little sketchy, but regardless of these facts, Miss Ragland kissed each of them over and over and smiled endlessly.

"Tell me who you are again," she would ask from time to time and again and again they would respond, "I am Edwards, this is Ogilvie, this is Simmons, and this is Woodson. We all worked with you at the Deerman County Sheriff's Department many years ago. We had some wonderful times together, Miss Ragland."

"I'm sure we did. I am so glad you girls came to see me today. I just love you all."

Another round of kisses were Miss Ragland's way of showing her love to each of them even though she didn't really remember who they were. While the visits from this point on were the same as this visit, the ladies did not stop their annual trek to see their friend, mentor, and loved one. Names had to be exchanged several more times before the end of the visit, but nobody minded. They all loved her unconditionally.

Never Can Say Goodbye

CHAPTER 37

These eight on ten rendezvous continued for another six years until October 2011. Edwards received a telephone call from Miss Ragland's daughter, Sandra. It seems that Miss Ragland passed away in her sleep. After listening to what Sandra was telling her, Edwards began to silently shed tears. A sadness came over her while all the time she was thinking about the good times they all had together but especially those times with their sergeant and friend, Miss Ragland.

"Mom's services have been scheduled for Friday, October 22, 2011, at the Grove Hill Funeral Home in Dallas, Texas. She wanted to be buried next to my dad Zachery and her mother, so that's what we will do. She had a good long life and she was happy when she passed. Would you please contact any county personnel you know that knew my mother and let them know about the services? Especially all of the deputies she worked with on the tenth floor."

"Sandra, I will be happy to," Edwards replied.

"Gigi, my whole family is grateful to you and the other ladies who always took time to visit my mom and always let her know how much you all cared for her even when she couldn't remember who you were."

All Edwards could do was reply in a soft teary voice, "We all truly loved her."

After gathering her composure and thoughts, Edwards did indeed call her comrades to let them know about Miss Ragland. Given the person who had the role of setting up all of the get-togethers for the group all of these past years, Simmons was the first person Edwards called. She was surprised and saddened by this news for many reasons but mainly because the group would not be able to see her again on their next upcoming visit. Pushing the tears aside to speak her comment was her normal response, "I will call everybody and let them know."

Soon the passing of Sgt. Ragland had spread throughout the county world. Many had made arrangements to attend her funeral services without question but especially her seven friends from the tenth floor. While all seven had plans to attend, Hill and Goodman were not able to change some plans already set. But cards and flowers were sent by all.

As expected, the nice size chapel at the Grove Hill Funeral Home was packed with well-wishers inside and out where there was standing room only. "I knew there would be a lot of people here today but people are still coming in," said Woodson.

"I know," responded Simmons. "She was a respected and well-liked and loved person. Just look at the words in her program: *"Generous, kind, and loving person and was loved by all who knew her."*

"I'm really going to miss her," said Astor. She always told me these stories about how she kept her marriage *fun and lively*, and it always amazed me. She did some things I couldn't believe. There was one story that involved a trampoline," laughed Astor. The ladies then started chiming in with those "do you remember" or "did she ever tell you" stories. It was a sad occasion that brought about smiles when speaking about her. I would suspect this is what a true definition of an adored person actually meant.

After the services, there were small groups convened throughout the chapel talking about Miss Ragland. There was no doubt that her two children, eight grandchildren, seventeen great grandchildren, and three great-great-grandchildren would miss her dearly. But her legacy lives on with them.

Needless to say that all future gatherings with the remaining seven on ten always had a conversation or two about Miss Ragland. These conversations all ended with smiles and fond memories of a woman who was loved by all. She is truly missed!

John 15:13

Greater love hath no man than this,

that a man lay down his life for his friends.

Proverbs 27:9

Ointment and perfume rejoice the heart: so doth the

sweetness of a man's friend by hearty counsel.

Sgt. Ragland　　Rita　Joy　Rose　Gigi　Laura　　Madyson　Poppi

Sgt. Ragle　　Renita　Jane　Ruby　Gail　Lana　　Marilyn　Pam

Look for book three in the Forever series, *Forever Stylish: Praying Clara coming soon*. The prelude, prologue, and Chapter 1 are shown below.

DEDICATION

I dedicate this book to my aunt, Corrie Wilson, who we call Aunt Sista.' She is a stylish and praying woman who always tells me that the Lord will always take care of our problems and to always trust in the Lord. I also have to thank her for using her seamstress skills to sew me a red, white, and blue window-paned four-piece pant suit all the way from Omaha, Nebraska. She did it just because she loved me. I was a budding teenager who just knew I looked good. I will never forget this pantsuit. Thank you Aunt Sista!

PRELUDE

To Young Clara,

Hello Clara. This letter is to the little six-year-old girl that literally grew up being a mother at the age of six, and this is your testimony. Through all of the tests and trials that you experienced in your young life, I can honestly say you became a better person, wife, mother, sibling, and daughter. When you were put in the role of being a mother to your brothers and sisters, you did not understand that this was a test that you passed. You didn't understand that our mother did the best that she could raising all of her children. She was just young with no knowledge of how to be a wife or mother. You did not understand then that being the oldest child in your family and the youngest mother to your siblings would help you to know what it meant to be a supportive mother to your seven children today.

I thank the Lord for guiding your steps and helping you make the choices that you did—some better than others—but nevertheless, helping you to be the Christian that you turned out to be today. If you had any regrets, I am sure it would be that you and your mother were not closer when you were growing up, but the Lord made sure that she is still in both of our lives. Thanks to you, I can't imagine my life without my entire family or the relationships that I have made in my seventy years on this earth. Thank you, Clara, for being you then and being me now.

Sincerely,
From Older Clara

PROLOGUE

*I*n this life there are so many uncertainties—uncertainties about one's health, about one's job status, about what our futures' hold, and about how other people can affect our lives. We all make plans about how we want our futures to unfold or the direction we want our lives to take. But because nothing in this life is certain except that the Lord died for our sins and that he loves us unconditionally, things will and do happen that are out of our control every day. In some instances, certain things that go on in a family change our thoughts on what we will and will not tolerate and how we choose to deal with the issues.

This is what happened in June 1953 to a six-year-old girl named Clara. Clara was put in a position that this six-year-old child never forgot but shaped the person that she became. Even though Clara was only six years old, she was smart beyond her years, and while she loved her family, she had already determined that the life she was going to have was going to be totally different than what she was experiencing thus far.

Can a six year old make a decision about their life? We will see as our story begins.

CHAPTER 1

"**W**ake up, Clara, wake up. I need for you to wake up and run as fast as you can to Mr. Harnell's farm. Tell Ms. Sue to come and help me deliver this baby coming. It's almost time. Hurry up Clara. *HURRY!!!!!*"

These were the words that Louise yelled that awakened her six-year-old daughter Clara from her well-deserved slumber. Little Clara had done a full day's work inside the house and whatever needed tending to outside of the house. These chores were part of her mother's quotidian directives to her each day. However, no chores were started before Clara said her morning prayers. She had to thank the Lord for her blessings and say a special prayer for her parents. Though her parents were not spiritual people nor did they attend church, Clara was born with a spiritual nature, and she knew from the time she could talk she was blessed and had to serve the Lord no matter what. She taught herself to pray and eventually read the Bible. She found out that prayer was the key to her happiness. This was reason enough for her to continue thanking her creator and Lord several times a day.

Clara immediately jumped from her small bed, put on her small stained pinafore, her oversized work boots with no laces, and ran out of the door. It was about nine o'clock P.M. on a hot night in June 1953 in the back woods of east Texas. Clara ran as fast as she could in the darkness, and she had no fear of the pitch black night air and sounds or what she had been asked to do.

Even in the darkness, it only took Clara a few minutes to get to the Harnell farm. When she arrived at the house, there were no visible lights showing, but that did not stop her from her assigned duties. When she got to the front door screen, she knocked and knocked.

"Miss Sue, Mama needs you. She is having her baby. Miss Sue, Miss Sue."

These pleas aroused movement in the house, and a light in the front room came on. Mr. Harnell came to the door and asked Clara what she needed. She proceeded to explain her mother needed his wife's help. In a few minutes, Miss Sue came out of the house fully dressed with a lamp, and the two headed back to Clara's house. As they entered the door, there was a loud scream coming from her mother's room. Miss Sue immediately went to Clara's mother assistance.

"I need a pan of hot water and some towels and sheets, Clara. You get the towels and sheets, and I will get the hot water," were Miss Sue's instructions.

Clara did not hesitate at completing her newly assigned task. The night was filled with screams and loud communication between patient and the midwife doctor. Clara, on the other hand, was nestled quietly in a corner of her bed anticipating the birth of another little brother or sister. She was already the big sister and mother of three younger siblings and another one on the way. While she didn't know it at this moment, she had one other brother who passed away the year after her birth.

Five hours later, Miss Sue came into Clara's room to see her sound asleep in an upright position leaning against the wall.

"Clara, wake up. You have a little sister," Miss Sue said to her.

A smile came across Clara's face, and Miss Sue ushered her into the room with her mother and little sister. She was now a big sister again, and she knew she would be the best big sister—and, she assumed, mother—ever. She thanked the Lord out loud for giving her this blessing, and Miss Sue heard her declaration to the Lord.

"My words. You are surely a praying child Clara. Good for you," are the words Miss Sue said after hearing her heartfelt prayers.

CPSIA information can be obtained
at www.ICGtesting.com
Printed in the USA
FSOW04n2319111017
39755FS